DIARY
of a
Wimpy Kid
RODRICK RULES

CRASH SMASH
BA-DUM BIDI BUM BOP
THUMP WHOMP

Whatever you do, don't ask Greg Heffley how he spent his summer holidays, because he definitely doesn't want to talk about it.

As Greg enters the new school year, he's eager to put the past three months behind him ... and one event in particular.

Unfortunately for Greg, his older brother Rodrick knows all about the incident. And secrets have a way of getting out ... especially when a diary is involved.

PUFFIN BOOKS

OTHER BOOKS BY JEFF KINNEY

DIARY
of a
Wimpy Kid

RODRICK RULES

by Jeff Kinney

PUFFIN BOOKS

PUFFIN BOOKS

Published by the Penguin Group
Penguin Group (Australia)
250 Camberwell Road
Camberwell, Victoria 3124, Australia
(a division of Pearson Australia Group Pty Ltd)
Penguin Group (USA) Inc.
375 Hudson Street, New York, New York 10014, USA
Penguin Group (Canada)
90 Eglinton Avenue East, Suite 700,
Toronto ON M4P 2Y3, Canada
(a division of Pearson Penguin Canada Inc.)
Penguin Books Ltd
80 Strand, London WC2R 0RL, England
Penguin Ireland
25 St Stephen's Green, Dublin 2, Ireland
(a division of Penguin Books Ltd)
Penguin Books India Pvt Ltd
11, Community Centre, Panchsheel Park, New Delhi-110 017, India
Penguin Group (NZ)
67 Apollo Drive, Rosedale, North Shore 0632, New Zealand
(a division of Pearson New Zealand Ltd)
Penguin Books (South Africa) (Pty) Ltd
24 Sturdee Avenue, Rosebank, Johannesburg 2196, South Africa

Penguin Books Ltd, Registered Offices: 80 Strand, London WC2R 0RL, England

First published in the English language in 2007 by Amulet Books (USA),
an imprint of Harry N. Abrams, Inc. New York
Original English title: Diary of a Wimpy Kid: Rodrick Rules (book two)
(All rights reserved in all countries by Harry N. Abrams, Inc.)
This edition published by Penguin Group (Australia), 2008

15 17 19 20 18 16

Text and illustrations copyright © 2009 Wimpy Kid, Inc.
DIARY OF A WIMPY KID®, WIMPY KID™, and the Greg Heffley design™
are trademarks of Wimpy Kid Inc. All rights reserved.
Cover design by Chad W. Beckerman and Jeff Kinney
Typeset in Wimpy Kid Regular
Printed in Australia by McPherson's Printing Group, Maryborough, Victoria

The moral right of the author/illustrator has been asserted.

National Library of Australia
Cataloguing-in-Publication data:

Kinney, Jeff.
Diary of a wimpy kid: Rodrick rules

ISBN 978 0 14 330384 8

1. Middle schools - Juvenile fiction. 2. Friendship -
Juvenile fiction. 3. Schools - Juvenile fiction. 4.
Diaries - Juvenile fiction. I. Title.

813.6

puffin.com.au

TO JULIE, WILL, AND GRANT

SEPTEMBER

Monday

I guess Mum was pretty proud of herself for making me write in that journal last year, because now she went and bought me another one.

But remember how I said that if some jerk caught me carrying a book with 'diary' on the cover they were gonna get the wrong idea? Well, that's exactly what happened today.

(MY BROTHER RODRICK)

Now that Rodrick knows I have another journal, I better remember to keep this one locked up. Rodrick actually got ahold of my LAST journal a few weeks back, and it was a disaster. But don't even get me started on THAT story.

Even without my Rodrick problems, my summer was pretty lousy.

Our family didn't go anywhere or do anything fun, and that's Dad's fault. Dad made me join the swim team again, and he wanted to make sure I didn't miss any meets this year.

Dad's got this idea that I'm destined to be a great swimmer or something, so that's why he makes me join the team every summer.

At my first swim meet a couple of years ago, Dad told me that when the umpire shot off the starter pistol, I was supposed to dive in and start swimming.

But what he DIDN'T tell me was that the starter gun only fired BLANKS.

So I was a whole lot more worried about where the bullet was gonna land than I was about getting myself to the other end of the pool.

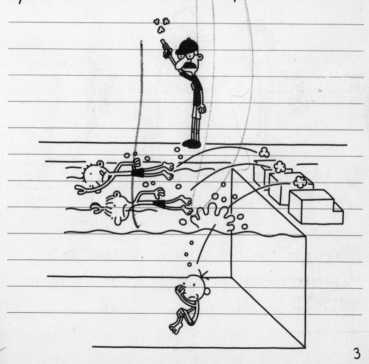

Even after Dad explained the whole 'starter pistol' concept to me, I was still the worst swimmer on the team.

But I did end up winning 'Most Improved' at the awards banquet at the end of the summer. That's only because there was a ten-minute difference between my first race and my last one.

So I guess Dad's still waiting for me to live up to my potential.

In a lot of ways, being on the swim team was worse than being in high school.

First of all, we had to be at the pool by 7.30 every morning, and the water was always FREEZING cold.

And second of all, we were all crammed into two lanes, so I always had somebody on my tail trying to get around me.

The reason we had to use two lanes was because swim practice was at the same time as the Water Jazz class.

I actually tried to convince Dad to let me do Water Jazz instead of swim team, but he wouldn't go for it.

COME ON, LADIES! GET THOSE ARMS UP!

This was the first summer the coach let us boys wear board shorts instead of those skimpy racing speedos. But Mum said Rodrick's hand-me-down speedos were 'perfectly fine'.

After swim practice, Rodrick would pick me up in his band's van. Mum had this crazy idea that if me and Rodrick spent 'quality time' on the ride home every day, we wouldn't fight as much. But all it did was make things a lot worse.

Rodrick was always half an hour late picking me up.

And he wouldn't let me sit up front. He said the chlorine would ruin his seat, even though the van is something like fifteen years old.

Rodrick's van doesn't actually have any seats in the back, so I had to squeeze in with all the band equipment. And every time the van came to a stop, I had to pray I didn't get my head taken off by one of Rodrick's drums.

I ended up walking home every day instead of getting a ride from Rodrick. I figured it was better to just walk the two miles than to get brain damage riding in the back of that van.

Halfway through the summer, I decided I was pretty much done with swim team. So I came up with a trick to get out of practice.

I'd swim a few laps, and then I'd ask the coach if I could use the bathroom. Then I'd just hide out in the locker room until practice was over.

The only problem with my plan was that it was something like forty degrees in the boys' bathroom. So it was even colder in THERE than it was in the pool.

I had to wrap myself up in toilet paper so I didn't get hypothermia.

That's how I spent a pretty big chunk of my summer holiday. And that's why I'm actually looking forward to going back to school tomorrow.

Tuesday
When I got to school today, everybody was acting all strange around me, and at first I didn't know WHAT was up.

Then I remembered: I still had the Cheese Touch from LAST year. I got the Cheese Touch in the last week of school, and over the summer I COMPLETELY forgot about it.

The problem with the Cheese Touch is that you've got it until you can pass it on to someone else. But nobody would even get within thirty feet of me, so I knew I was gonna be stuck with the Cheese Touch for the whole school year.

Luckily, there was a new kid named Jeremy Pindle in homeroom, so that took care of THAT problem.

My first class was Pre-Algebra, and the teacher put me right next to Alex Aruda, the smartest kid in the whole class.

Alex is SUPER easy to copy off of, because he always finishes his test early and puts his paper down on the floor next to him. So if I ever get in a pinch, it's nice to know I can count on Alex to bail me out.

Kids whose last names start with the first few letters of the alphabet get called on the most by the teacher, and that's why they end up being the smartest.

Some people think that's not true, but if you want to come down to my school, I can prove it.

ALEX ARUDA   CHRISTOPHER ZIEGEL

I can only think of ONE kid who broke the last-name rule, and that's Peter Uteger. Peter was the smartest kid in the class all the way up until the fifth grade.

That's when a bunch of us started giving him a hard time about how his initials sounded when you said them out loud.

These days, Peter doesn't raise his hand at ALL, and he's pretty much a C student.

I guess I feel a little bad about the whole P.U. thing and what happened to Peter. But it's hard not to take credit whenever it comes up.

Anyway, today I got pretty decent seats in all my classes except seventh-period History. My teacher is Mr Huff, and something tells me he had Rodrick as a student a few years back.

> MR HEFFLEY, YOU'LL BE SITTING IN THIS CHAIR NEXT TO MY DESK.

Wednesday

Mum has been making me and Rodrick help out more around the house, and now the two of us are responsible for doing the dishes every night.

The rule is that we're not allowed to watch any TV or play video games until all the dishes are done. But let me just say that Rodrick is the WORST dishes partner in the world.

As soon as dinner is over, he goes upstairs to the bathroom and camps out there for an hour. And by the time he comes back downstairs, I'm already done.

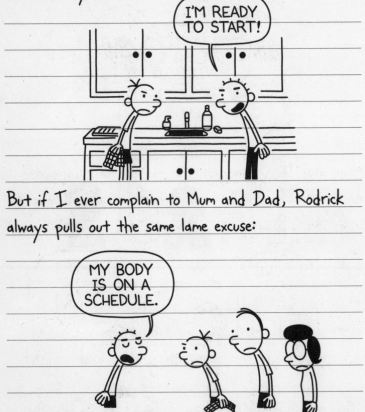

But if I ever complain to Mum and Dad, Rodrick always pulls out the same lame excuse:

I think Mum and Dad are too worried about my little brother, Manny, to get involved in a fight between me and Rodrick right now anyway.

Yesterday, Manny drew a picture at day care, and Mum and Dad got really upset when they found it in his backpack.

Mum and Dad thought the picture was supposed to be of THEM, so now they're acting all lovey in front of Manny.

I knew who it was REALLY supposed to be in the picture: me and Rodrick.

We got into a big blowout over the remote control the other night, and Manny was there to witness the whole thing. But Mum and Dad don't need to find out about THAT.

Thursday
Another reason my summer was kind of lame was because my best friend, Rowley, was on holiday pretty much the whole time. I think he went to South America or something, but to be honest with you, I'm not really sure.

I don't know if this makes me a bad person or whatever, but it's hard for me to get interested in other people's holidays.

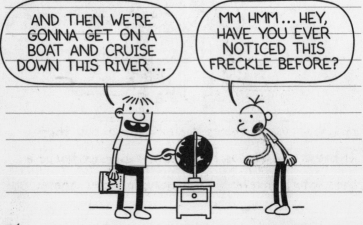

AND THEN WE'RE GONNA GET ON A BOAT AND CRUISE DOWN THIS RIVER...

MM HMM... HEY, HAVE YOU EVER NOTICED THIS FRECKLE BEFORE?

Besides, it seems like Rowley's family is always travelling to some crazy place in the world, and I can never keep their trips straight.

The other reason I don't care about Rowley's trips is because whenever Rowley comes back from one of his holidays, he always crams it down my throat.

Last year, Rowley and his family went to Australia for ten days, but from the way he acted when he got back, you'd think he lived there his whole life.

G'DAY, MATE!

Another thing that's really annoying is that whenever Rowley goes to some new country, he gets into whatever fad is going on over there.

Like when Rowley got back from Europe two years ago, he got hooked on this pop singer named 'Joshie', who I guess is some huge star or something. So Rowley came back with his bags full of Joshie CDs and posters and stuff.

I took one look at the picture on the CD and told Rowley that Joshie was supposed to be for six-year-old girls, but he didn't believe me. Rowley said I was just jealous because he was the one who 'discovered' Joshie.

And what made it really irritating was that now this guy was Rowley's new hero. So if I ever tried to say anything critical at all, Rowley didn't want to hear it.

Speaking of foreign countries, today in French class, Madame Lefrere told us we're going to be choosing pen pals this year.

When Rodrick was in high school, he had a seventeen-year-old girl from Holland as his pen pal. I know because I've seen the letters in his junk drawer.

When Madame Lefrere handed out the forms, I made sure I checked off the boxes that would get me a pen pal just like Rodrick's.

But after Madame Lefrere read over my form, she made me start over and pick again. She said I had to choose a boy who is my age, AND he has to be French. So I don't exactly have high hopes for my pen-pal experience.

Friday
Mum decided to start making Rodrick pick me up after school, just like he picked me up after swim practice. I guess that means she didn't learn from THAT experience. But I did. So when Rodrick picked me up today, I asked him to please take it easy on the brakes.

Rodrick said OK, but then he went out of his way to find every speed bump in town.

When I got out of the van, I called Rodrick a big jerk, and then it got physical. Mum saw the whole thing unfold from the living room window.

Mum made us come inside, and she sat us down at the kitchen table. Then she said me and Rodrick were going to have to settle our differences in a 'civil manner'.

Mum told me and Rodrick we each had to write down what we did wrong, and then we had to draw a picture to go along with it. And I knew exactly where Mum was going with THAT idea.

Mum used to be a preschool teacher, and whenever a kid would do something wrong, she'd make him draw a picture of it. I guess the idea was to make the kid feel ashamed of what he did so he wouldn't do it again.

I will not break the crayons because that makes the other children very sad.

Well, Mum's idea might have worked great on a bunch of four-year-olds, but she's going to have to think of something better if she wants me and Rodrick to get along.

The truth is, Rodrick can pretty much treat me any way he wants, because he knows there's nothing I can do about it.

See, Rodrick is the only one who knows about this REALLY embarrassing thing that happened to me over the summer, and he's been holding it over my head ever since. So if I ever tell on him for anything, he'll spill my secret to the whole world.

I just wish I had some dirt on HIM to even things out.

I do know ONE embarrassing thing about Rodrick, but I don't think it's gonna do me any good.

When Rodrick was a sophomore, he was sick the day they did school photos. So Mum told Dad to mail in Rodrick's freshman picture for the school to use in the yearbook.

Don't ask me how Dad screwed this up, but he sent in Rodrick's SECOND-grade picture.

And believe it or not, it actually got printed.

| Harrington, Leonard | Hatley, Andrew | Heffley, Rodrick | Hills, Heather |

Unfortunately, Rodrick was smart enough to rip that page out of his yearbook. So if I'm ever gonna find something to use against him, I guess I have to keep digging.

Wednesday

Ever since Mum assigned the dishes to me and Rodrick, Dad's been going down to the furnace room after dinner to work on this miniature Civil War battlefield of his.

Dad spends at least three hours a night down there working on that thing. I think Dad would be happy to spend the whole weekend working on his battlefield, but Mum has OTHER plans for him.

Mum likes to rent these romantic comedies, and she makes Dad watch them with her. But I know Dad is just waiting for the first chance to break away and go back down to the basement.

Whenever Dad can't be down in the furnace room, he makes sure us kids keep away from it.

Dad won't let me or Rodrick go NEAR his battlefield, because he thinks we're gonna mess something up.

And earlier today I overheard Dad say something to Manny to make sure HE doesn't go poking around back there, either.

Saturday

Rowley came over to my house today. Dad doesn't like it when Rowley comes over, because Dad always says Rowley is 'accident prone'. I think it's because this one time Rowley was eating dinner here, and he dropped a plate and broke it.

So now Dad has this idea that Rowley is going to ruin his whole Civil War battlefield in one klutzy move.

Whenever Rowley comes over to my house these days, he gets the same greeting:

Rowley's dad doesn't like ME, either. That's why I don't go over to his house much any more.

The last time I spent the night at Rowley's, we watched this movie where some kids taught themselves a secret language that no grown-ups could understand.

TRANSLATION: AT EXACTLY 2.30 P.M., LET'S ALL DROP OUR BOOKS ON THE FLOOR.

Me and Rowley thought that was pretty cool, and we tried to figure out how to talk in the same language the kids were using in the movie.

But we couldn't really get the hang of it, so we made up our OWN secret language.

Then we tried it out at dinner.

But Rowley's dad must have cracked our code, because I ended up getting sent home before dessert. And I haven't been invited to spend the night at Rowley's ever since.

When Rowley came over to my house today, he brought a bunch of pictures from his trip with him. He said the best part of his holiday was when they went on a river safari, and he showed me all these blurry pictures of birds and stuff.

Now, I've been to the Wild Kingdom amusement park a bunch of times, and they have this River Rapids ride where they have these awesome robot animals like gorillas and dinosaurs.

If you ask me, Rowley's parents should have just saved their money and taken him there instead.

DID YOU SEE ANY SHARKS FIGHTING GIANT TARANTULAS ON YOUR SAFARI?

NO. AND SHARKS DON'T FIGHT TARANTULAS.

WELL, AT WILD KINGDOM THEY DO.

But of course Rowley didn't want to hear about MY experiences, so he just gathered up his pictures and went back home.

Tonight after dinner, Mum made Dad watch one of the movies she rented, but Dad really wanted to work on his Civil War battlefield.

When Mum got up to go to the bathroom, Dad stuffed a bunch of pillows under the blanket on his side of the bed to make it look like he was asleep.

Mum didn't find out about Dad's decoy until after the movie was over.

She made Dad come to bed, even though it was only 8.30.

And now Manny sleeps in Mum and Dad's bed, because he's afraid of the monster that lives in the furnace room.

Tuesday

I thought I was done hearing about Rowley's trip, but I was wrong. Yesterday, our Social Studies teacher asked Rowley to tell the class all about his holiday, and today he came to school wearing this ridiculous costume. But what was even WORSE was when some girls came up to Rowley at lunch and started kissing his butt.

But then I realised maybe that wasn't such a bad thing after all. So I started parading Rowley around the cafeteria, because after all, he IS my best friend.

Saturday
Dad has been taking me to the mall every Saturday for the past few weeks. At first, I thought it was because he wanted to spend more time with me. But then I realised he's just making sure he's out of the house for Rodrick's band practices, which I can totally understand.

Rodrick and his heavy-metal band practise in the basement on weekends.

The lead singer of the band is this guy named
Bill Walter, and me and Dad bumped into Bill on
the way out the door today.

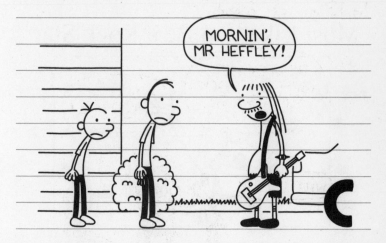

Bill doesn't have a job, and he still lives with his
parents, even though he's thirty-five years old.

I'm pretty sure Dad's worst fear is that
Rodrick is going to see Bill as some kind of role
model, and that Rodrick will want to follow in
Bill's footsteps.

So whenever Dad sees Bill, it just puts him in a
bad mood for the rest of the day.

The reason Rodrick invited Bill to be in his band was because Bill got voted 'Most Likely to Be a Rock Star' when HE was in high school.

Most Likely to Be a Rock Star

Bill Walter   Anna Wrentham

That hasn't really worked out for Bill yet. And I think I heard Anna Wrentham is in prison.

Anyway, me and Dad went to the mall for a few hours today, but when we got back, Rodrick's band practice wasn't over yet. You could hear the guitars and drums from a block away, and there were a bunch of random teenagers hanging out in our driveway.

I guess they must have heard the music coming
out of the basement and got drawn to it, sort
of like how moths get drawn to a light.

When Dad saw all those teenagers in the driveway,
he TOTALLY freaked out.

Dad ran inside to call the cops, but Mum stopped
him before he could dial 000.

Mum said those teenagers weren't doing any harm,
and that they were just 'appreciating' Rodrick's
music. But I don't even know how she could say
that with a straight face. And if you ever heard
Rodrick's band, you'd know what I mean.

Dad couldn't relax with all those teenagers out in our driveway.

So Dad went upstairs and got his boom box. Then he put in a classical music CD and let it play. And you would not BELIEVE how quickly the driveway cleared out after that.

Dad was pretty proud of himself for thinking up that one. But Mum accused him of getting rid of Rodrick's 'fans' on purpose.

Sunday
Today, on the car ride to church, I was making faces at Manny, trying to get him to laugh. I made this one face that made Manny laugh so hard that apple juice came out of his nose.

But then Mum said:

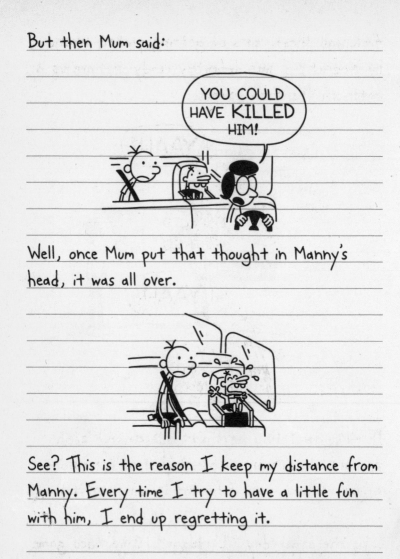

YOU COULD HAVE **KILLED** HIM!

Well, once Mum put that thought in Manny's head, it was all over.

See? This is the reason I keep my distance from Manny. Every time I try to have a little fun with him, I end up regretting it.

I remember when I was younger, and Mum and Dad told me I was getting a little brother. I was REALLY excited.

After all those years of getting pushed around by Rodrick, I was definitely ready to move up a notch on the totem pole.

But Mum and Dad have always been SUPER protective of Manny, and they won't let me lay a finger on him, even if he totally deserves it.

Like the other day, I plugged in my video game system, and it wouldn't start. I opened it up and found out that Manny had stuffed a chocolate-chip cookie in the disc drive.

And of course Manny used the same excuse he ALWAYS uses when he breaks my stuff.

I really wanted to let Manny have it, but I couldn't do anything with Mum standing right there.

Mum said she would have a 'talk' with Manny, and they went downstairs. Half an hour later, they came back up to my room, and Manny was holding something in his hands.

It was a ball of tinfoil with a bunch of toothpicks
sticking out of it.

Don't ask me how that was supposed to make
up for my broken video game system. I went to
throw the stupid thing away, but Mum wouldn't
even let me do THAT.

The first chance I get, that thing's going in the
trash. Because mark my words, if I don't get rid
of it, I'm gonna end up sitting on it.

Even though Manny drives me totally nuts, there is ONE reason I like having him around. Ever since Manny started talking, Rodrick has stopped making me sell chocolate bars for his school fund-raisers. And believe me, I'm grateful for THAT.

BEFORE...

NOW...

Monday
Madame Lefrere made us write our first pen-pal
letters today. I got assigned to this kid named
Mamadou Montpierre, and I guess he lives
someplace in France.

I know I'm supposed to write in French and
Mamadou is supposed to write in English, but to
be honest with you, writing in a foreign language
is pretty hard.

So I really don't see the need for both of us to
stress out over this whole pen-pal thing.

> Dear Mamadou,
>
> First of all, I think we should both
> just write in English to keep things simple.

By the way, remember how I said I was gonna
end up sitting on Manny's spiky tinfoil ball thing?
Well, I was half right.

45

Rowley came over today to play video games, and HE ended up sitting on it.

I'm actually kind of relieved, to be honest with you. I lost track of that thing a couple of days ago, and I'm just glad it finally turned up.

And in all the commotion, I threw Manny's 'gift' in the garbage. But something tells me Mum wouldn't have stopped me this time.

Wednesday
Rodrick has an English paper due tomorrow, and Mum's actually making him do it himself for once. Rodrick doesn't know how to type, so he usually writes his papers out on notebook paper and then hands them off to Dad.

46

But when Dad reads over Rodrick's work, he finds all sorts of factual errors.

Rodrick doesn't really care about the mistakes, so he tells Dad to just go ahead and type the paper like it is.

But Dad can't stand typing a paper with errors in it, so he just rewrites Rodrick's paper from scratch. And then a couple of days later, Rodrick brings his graded paper home and acts like he did it himself.

This has been going on for a few years, and I guess Mum decided she's going to put an end to it. So tonight she told Dad that Rodrick was going to have to do his OWN work this time around, and that Dad wasn't allowed to help out.

Rodrick went in the computer room after dinner, and you could hear him typing about one letter a minute.

I could tell the sound of Rodrick typing was driving Dad totally bananas. On top of that, Rodrick would come out of the computer room every ten minutes and ask Dad some dumb question.

WHERE'S THE SPACE BAR AGAIN?

After a couple of hours, Dad finally cracked.

Dad waited for Mum to go to bed, and then he typed Rodrick's whole paper for him. So I guess this means Rodrick's system is safe, at least for now.

I have a book report due tomorrow, but I'm really not sweating it.

I found the secret to doing book reports a long time ago. I've been milking the same book for the past five years: 'Sherlock Sammy Does It Again.'

There are about twenty short stories in 'Sherlock Sammy Does It Again', but I just treat each story like it's a whole book, and the teacher never notices.

These Sherlock Sammy stories are all the same. Some grown-up commits a crime, and then Sherlock Sammy figures it out and makes the person look stupid.

I'm kind of an expert at writing book reports by now. All you have to do is write exactly what the teacher wants to hear, and you're all set.

Man, Sherlock Sammy is
so smart, and I'll bet that's
cause he reads so many
books.

I'll bet you're right!

There were a bunch of
hard words in this book,
but I looked them up in
the dictionary so now I
know what they mean.

*I guess you're a
bit of a "sleuth"
yourself!* (A+)

OCTOBER

<u>Monday</u>

There was a kid named Chirag Gupta who was one of my friends last year, but he moved away in June. His family had a big going-away party, and the whole neighbourhood came. But I guess Chirag's family must have changed their mind, because today Chirag was back in school.

Everyone was happy to see Chirag again, but a couple of us decided to have a little fun with him before officially welcoming him back.

So we basically pretended he was still gone.

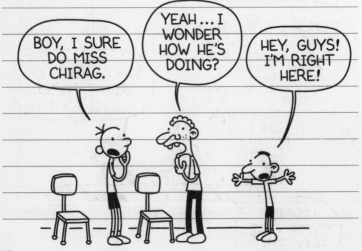

I have to admit, it was pretty funny.

DID YOU JUST HEAR SOMETHING?

NOPE... MUST HAVE BEEN THE WIND!

!

At lunch, Chirag sat next to me. I had an extra chocolate-chip cookie in my lunch bag, and I made a big deal about it.

I WISH CHIRAG WAS HERE. OH, HOW HE LOVED CHOCOLATE-CHIP COOKIES.

BUT I'M SITTING RIGHT NEXT TO YOU!

I'M NOT EVEN THAT HUNGRY...

OK, so maybe that one was a little cruel.

(GOBBLE GOBBLE
SMACK SMACK)

I guess we'll probably let Chirag off the hook tomorrow. But then again, this Invisible Chirag thing could turn into the next 'P.U.'

Tuesday
OK, so the Invisible Chirag joke is still going, and the whole CLASS is in on it now. I don't want to get too far ahead of myself or any-thing, but I think I might have Class Clown in the bag for dreaming this one up.

In Science, the teacher asked me to count the number of kids in the classroom so she'd know how many pairs of safety goggles to get out of the closet.

So I made a big show of counting everyone in the room except Chirag.

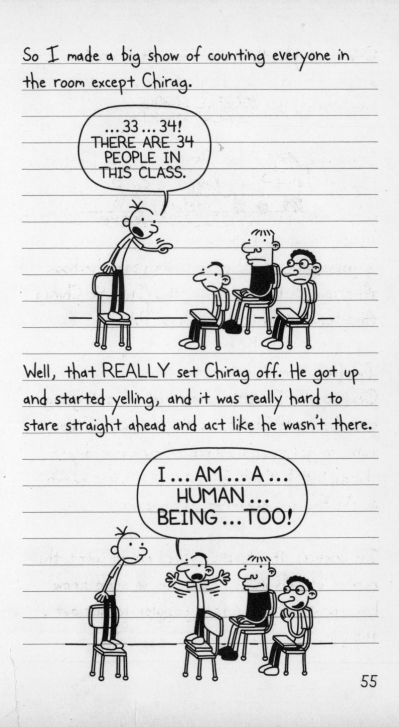

Well, that REALLY set Chirag off. He got up and started yelling, and it was really hard to stare straight ahead and act like he wasn't there.

I wanted to tell him that we never said he wasn't a human being, it's just that he's an INVISIBLE human being. But I managed to keep my mouth shut.

Before you go and say I'm a bad friend for teasing Chirag, let me just say this in my own defence: I'm smaller than about 95% of the kids at my school, so when it comes to finding someone I can actually pick on, my options are pretty limited.

And besides, I'm not 100% to blame for dreaming up this idea. Believe it or not, I got the idea from Mum. This one time when I was a kid, I was playing under the kitchen table, and Mum came looking for me.

HAS ANYONE SEEN GREGORY?

I don't know what made me do it, but I decided
to play a joke on Mum and stay hidden.

Mum went all around the house calling my name.
I think she must have finally seen me under the
kitchen table, but she still pretended she didn't
know where I was.

I thought it was pretty funny, and I probably
would've stayed hidden under there for a little
while more. But Mum finally got me to crack when
she said she was gonna give my gum-ball machine
to Rodrick.

So if you want to point fingers on the Invisible Chirag joke, now you know who's really to blame.

Thursday

Well, yesterday, Chirag pretty much gave up on trying to get anyone in our class to talk to him.

But today he found our weakness.

ROWLEY, DO **YOU** THINK I EXIST?

NOPE! I CAN'T EVEN HEAR YOU OR SEE YOU!

I forgot ALL about Rowley. When the joke first started up, I made sure to keep him away from Chirag, because I had a feeling Rowley would blow the joke.

But I guess I kind of got too cocky and let my guard down.

Chirag started working on Rowley at lunch, and he came really close to getting him to crack.

IF YOU SAY I EXIST, THIS CORN DOG IS YOURS!

I could tell Rowley was about to say something, so I had to act quick. I told everyone there was a floating corn dog hovering above our lunch table, and then I plucked it out of the air and ate it in two bites.

So thanks to my quick thinking, we were able to keep the joke going.

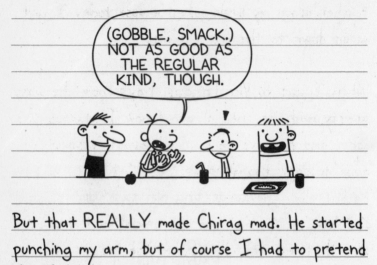

But that REALLY made Chirag mad. He started punching my arm, but of course I had to pretend like I didn't notice.

And let me tell you, that wasn't easy to do. Chirag might be small, but that kid can really punch.

Friday

Well, I guess Chirag must have complained to a teacher about my little joke, because today I got called down to the front office.

When I got to Vice Principal Roy's room, he was pretty mad. He knew all about how I started the joke, and he gave me a speech about 'respect' and 'decency' and all that.

But luckily, Mr Roy got one crucial fact wrong, and that was the identity of the person we were playing the joke on. So that made the apology part a whole lot easier.

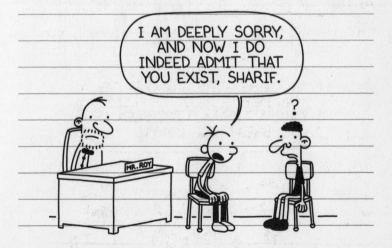

I AM DEEPLY SORRY, AND NOW I DO INDEED ADMIT THAT YOU EXIST, SHARIF.

Mr Roy seemed pretty satisfied with my apology, and he let me go without even tacking on any detention.

I've always heard that when Mr Roy is done chewing a kid out, he sends them off with a pat on the back and a lollipop. And now I can tell you firsthand that it's true.

Saturday
Rowley's birthday party is tomorrow, so Mum took me to the mall to get him a gift. I picked out this cool video game that just came out, and I handed it to Mum so she could pay for it. But Mum said I had to buy it with my OWN money.

I told Mum that first of all, I have zero money.

And second of all, if I DID have any money, I wouldn't be wasting it on ROWLEY.

Mum didn't seem too happy with what I said, but it's not MY fault I'm broke. I actually had a job this summer, but the people I worked for stiffed me, so I didn't earn a single penny.

We have these neighbours named the Fullers who live a few doors up, and they go away on holiday every summer.

They usually leave their dog, Princess, in the kennel, but this year, they told me they'd pay me five bucks a day to feed Princess and take her out. I figured I'd earn enough to buy a whole pile of video games with that kind of money.

But I guess Princess is gun-shy about going to the bathroom in front of strangers, so I ended up spending a lot of time standing around in the hot sun waiting for this dumb dog to hurry up and go.

I'd wait and wait and nothing would happen, and then I'd just take Princess back inside.

But EVERY time I'd leave, Princess would make a big mess in the foyer, and I'd have to clean it up the next day. Toward the end of the summer I got smart and realised it would be a whole lot easier to just clean up all of Princess's messes at once instead of doing it every single day.

So I fed her and let her do her business on the foyer floor for about two weeks.

Then, the day before the Fullers were due back, I headed up the hill with all my cleaning supplies.

But guess what? The Fullers cut their trip short and got home a day EARLY.

I guess they didn't know it's polite to call ahead and let people know when your plans have changed.

Tonight, Mum called a house meeting with me and Rodrick. She said that the two of us are always complaining that we don't have any money, so she came up with a way for us to earn some cash.

Then she pulled out some play money she must've dug up out of a board game, and she called the money 'Mum Bucks'. Mum said we could earn Mum Bucks by doing chores and good deeds and stuff like that, and we could trade them in for REAL money.

Mum handed us $1,000 each to get us started. I thought I had struck it rich. But then she explained that each Mum Buck was only worth one cent of REAL money.

Mum told us how we should save up our Mum Bucks, and if we were patient, we could buy something we really wanted.

But Rodrick cashed in his whole stash before Mum was even done talking.

Then he went down to the convenience store and blew his money on some heavy-metal magazines.

If Rodrick wants to waste his money like that, he can go right ahead. But I'm gonna be smart with MY Mum Bucks.

Sunday
Today was Rowley's birthday party, and he had it at the mall. I'm sure I would have thought it was a lot of fun if I was about seven years old.

That was the average age of the kids at Rowley's party. Rowley invited his whole karate team, and most of those kids are still in primary school. I just wish I would have known what the party was gonna be like so I could have skipped it.

We started off playing these dopey party games like Pin the Tail on the Donkey and stuff like that. The last game we played was Hide-and-Seek.

My plan was to just hide in the ball pit and stay there until the party was over. But some OTHER kid was already in there.

It turned out this kid wasn't from Rowley's party. He was from the LAST birthday party that happened an hour earlier.

I guess he must have hid in there during Hide-and-Seek, and nobody ever FOUND him.

So Rowley's party had to be put on hold while the staff tried to track down this kid's parents.

After that situation got cleared up, we had cake and watched Rowley open his gifts. He mostly got a bunch of kids' toys, but he seemed pretty happy about it.

Then Rowley's parents gave him their present.
And guess what? It was a DIARY.

It kind of ticked me off, because I knew
Rowley asked his parents for a diary so he could
be just like me. After Rowley opened his present
he said:

I let him know exactly what I thought of that
idea by slugging him in the arm. And I really
don't care that it was his birthday, either.

One thing I will say, though. I used to be mad at Mum for getting me a journal that looked too girly. But after seeing Rowley's diary, I'm not so mad anymore.

Lately, Rowley has been TOTALLY riding me. He reads the same comic books I read, drinks the same kind of soda I drink, you name it. Mum says I should be 'flattered', but to be honest with you, it's totally creeping me out.

A couple days ago, I did an experiment to see just how far Rowley would go.

I rolled up one of my pant legs and tied a bandanna around my ankle and went to school that way.

Sure enough, the next day Rowley came to school wearing the same exact thing.

And that's how I ended up in Vice Principal Roy's office for the second time in a week.

THERE ARE SOME THUGS OUTSIDE MY HOUSE SPORTING 'GANG COLORS'.

Monday
I thought I was totally in the clear for the Invisible Chirag thing. But, boy, was I wrong.

Tonight, Mum got a call from Chirag's DAD. Mr Gupta told Mum all about the prank we were playing on his son, and how I was the ringleader.

When Mum questioned me, I told her I didn't even know what Chirag's dad was talking about.

Then Mum marched me up to Rowley's house to hear what HE had to say.

Luckily, I was prepared for this kind of thing. I had already drilled Rowley on what to do if we ever got busted, and that if we both just denied everything, we'd be OK.

But the second Mum started asking Rowley
questions, he broke down.

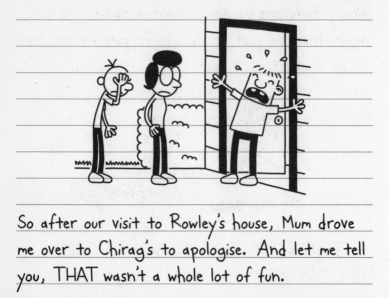

So after our visit to Rowley's house, Mum drove
me over to Chirag's to apologise. And let me tell
you, THAT wasn't a whole lot of fun.

Mr Gupta didn't seem too impressed with my
apology, but believe it or not, Chirag was actually
pretty cool about it.

After I apologised, Chirag invited me inside to play video games. I think he was so relieved to finally have one of his classmates talking to him again that he just decided to forgive me for the whole incident.

So I guess I forgive him, too.

Tuesday
Even though Chirag let me off the hook last night, Mum wasn't done with me yet.

She wasn't really that mad about the joke or how I treated Chirag. She was just mad that I LIED about it.

So Mum told me she'll ground me for a MONTH if she catches me lying again.

And that means I better watch my step, because Mum's not gonna forget what she said. When it comes to my screwups, Mum has a memory like an elephant.

THAT'S THE SECOND TIME YOU TRACKED MUD INTO THE KITCHEN!

(FIRST TIME: SIX YEARS AGO)

Last year Mum caught me lying, and I paid the price for it.

Mum made a gingerbread house a week before Christmas, and she put it on top of the fridge. She said nobody was allowed to touch it until Christmas Eve dinner.

But I couldn't help myself. So every night, I
snuck downstairs and picked off a little piece of
the gingerbread house. I tried to only eat a tiny
piece each time so Mum wouldn't notice.

It was really hard to limit myself to one gumdrop
or one little crumb of gingerbread each night, but
I managed to do it anyway.

I didn't know how much I had actually eaten until Mum took it down off the fridge on Christmas Eve.

When Mum accused me of eating all the candy, I denied it. But I wish I just fessed up right away, because that fib totally backfired on me.

Mum had just gotten hired to write a parenting column for the local newspaper, and she was always looking for material. So that incident pretty much made me into a local celebrity.

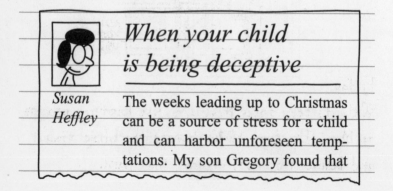

When your child is being deceptive

Susan Heffley

The weeks leading up to Christmas can be a source of stress for a child and can harbor unforeseen temptations. My son Gregory found that

You know, now that I think about it, Mum isn't exactly squeaky clean when it comes to being honest HERSELF.

I remember when I was a kid, and she found out I wasn't brushing my teeth every night. She faked a call to the dentist's office. And that call is the reason why I still brush my teeth four times a day.

Friday

Well, it's been three days and I've kept my promise to Mum. I've been 100% honest the whole time, and believe it or not, it's not that hard.

In fact, it's kind of liberating. I've been in a couple of situations already where I was a lot more honest than I would have been a week ago.

For example, the other day I had a conversation with this neighbourhood kid named Shawn Snella.

And yesterday, Rowley's family had a birthday party for his grandfather.

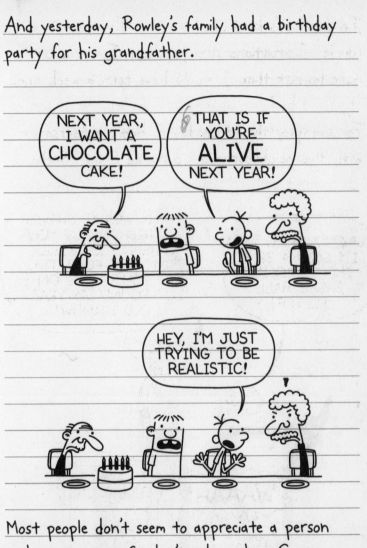

Most people don't seem to appreciate a person as honest as me. So don't ask me how George Washington ever got to be president.

Saturday

Today I answered the phone, and it was Mrs Gillman from the PTA, looking for Mum. I tried to hand her the phone, but she whispered for me to tell Mrs Gillman that she wasn't home.

I couldn't tell if Mum was trying to trick me into lying or WHAT, but there was no way I was going to break my honesty streak over something as dumb as THIS.

So I made Mum go out on the front porch before I said a word to Mrs Gillman.

MY MOTHER IS NOT INSIDE THE HOUSE RIGHT NOW.

And from the look Mum gave me when she came back in the house, I kind of get the feeling she's not gonna hold me to that honesty pledge any more.

Monday

Today was Career Day at school. They have Career Day every year to get us kids to start thinking about our future.

They brought in a bunch of adults who had all these different jobs. I think the idea is that us kids will find out about a job we like, and then we'll know what we want to be when we grow up.

But what REALLY happens is that you just find out which jobs to rule out.

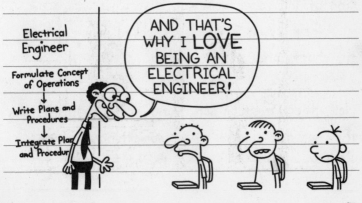

After the presentations, we had to fill out these questionnaires. The first question was, 'Where do you see yourself in fifteen years?'

I know EXACTLY where I'll be in fifteen years: in my pool, at my mansion, counting my money. But there weren't any check boxes for THAT option.

The questionnaires are supposed to predict what kind of job you're going to have when you grow up. When I was finished, I looked up my job on the chart, and I got 'Clerk'.

Well, there must be something wrong with the way they set these forms up or something, because I don't know any clerks who are billionaires.

Some other kids were unhappy with the jobs they ended up with, too. But the teacher said we shouldn't take these things too seriously.

Well, try telling that to Edward Mealey. Last year he got 'Sanitation Worker' on his job chart, and the teachers have been treating him different ever since.

EDWARD, COULD YOU PLEASE CLEAN UP THIS JUICE SPILL?

SCOOT SCOOT

Rowley got 'Nurse' on his job chart, and he seemed pretty happy about it. A couple of girls got Nurse, too, and they were chatting away with Rowley after class.

Next year I have to remember to sit next to Rowley and copy his job form so I can get in on some of that action.

Saturday
Me and Rodrick were just sitting around the house today, so Mum sent us over to Gramma's to rake her leaves.

Mum said she'd pay us $100 in Mum Bucks for each bag we filled. Plus, Gramma said she'd give us hot chocolate after we were finished.

I really didn't feel like working on a Saturday, but I needed the cash. Besides, Gramma makes really awesome hot chocolate. So we got some rakes and plastic bags from our garage and headed down to Gramma's house.

I took one side of the yard, and Rodrick took the other. But ten minutes into the job, Rodrick came over and told me I was doing everything all wrong.

Rodrick said I was putting WAY too many leaves in each bag, and that if I just tied the bag closer to the bottom, I could get done a lot quicker.

See, now this is the kind of advice you're SUPPOSED to get from your older brother.

After Rodrick showed me that trick, we went through bags like nobody's business. In fact, we ran out in half an hour.

Gramma didn't seem too happy about forking over the hot chocolate when we came inside. But like they say, a deal's a deal.

AHHHH!

Monday
Ever since Career Day, Rowley has been spending lunch with a bunch of girls who sit at the corner table in the cafeteria. I guess the group of them is like the Future Nurses of America or something.

Don't ask me WHAT they talk about over there.
They just whisper and giggle like a bunch of
first-graders.

All I can say is, they better not be talking
about ME.

You remember how I said Rodrick is the only one
who knows about that really embarrassing thing
that happened to me over the summer? Well,
Rowley knows the SECOND most embarrassing
thing that ever happened to me, and I really
don't need him digging it back up.

Back in fifth grade, we had a project in Spanish
where we had to do a skit in front of the class,
and my partner was Rowley.

We had to do the whole skit in Spanish. Rowley asked me what I would do for a candy bar, and I said I'd stand on my head.

But when I tried to do a headstand, I tipped over, and my rear end went right through the wall.

Well, the school never bothered to fix the hole, so for the rest of my time in primary school, my butt-print was on display in Mrs Gonzales's room.

And if Rowley's spreading that story around, believe me I'm gonna tell the whole world who ate the Cheese.

Wednesday

Today I realised that if I wanted to know what
Rowley and those girls are talking about at lunch,
all I have to do is read his DIARY. I'll bet he's
writing down all sorts of juicy gossip in that thing.

The problem is, Rowley's diary is LOCKED. So
even if I got ahold of it, I wouldn't have any way
to open it. But then I thought of something. All
I had to do was buy the same exact diary HE
has, and then I'd have a key.

So I went to the bookstore tonight and got
the last one on the shelf. I just hope buying
this thing was worth it, because I had to cash
in half of my Mum Bucks to pay for it. And I
don't think Dad was too thrilled with the idea of
me buying a Sweet Secrets Diary, either.

Thursday

After Phys Ed today, I saw that Rowley accidentally left his diary on the bench. So when the coast was clear, I used my new key on his diary, and sure enough, it worked.

I opened it up and started reading.

Dear Diary,

Today I played with my Dinoblazer action figures again. It was Mecharex vs. Triceraclops and Mecharex bited Triceraclops in the tail.

OW! DARN.

And then Triceraclops
turned around and
said oh yeah well how
do you like _that_ and
he shot Mecharex right
in the heinie.

OW NO FAIR.

I flipped through the rest of the book to see if
my name was in there anywhere, but it was just
page after page of this garbage.

After seeing what's going on in Rowley's head,
I'm kind of starting to wonder why I'm even
friends with him in the first place.

Saturday
Things at home have been really good for about
a week. Rodrick has the flu, so he doesn't have
the energy to bother me. And Manny has been
at Gramma's, so I've had the TV all to myself.

Yesterday, Mum and Dad made a surprise announcement. They said they were going away for the night, and that me and Rodrick were in charge of the house.

That was some pretty big news, because Mum and Dad have NEVER left me and Rodrick on our own before.

I think they've always been afraid that if they go away, Rodrick is gonna have a huge party and trash the house.

But with Rodrick knocked out with the flu, they must've seen their big chance. So after Mum gave us a speech about 'responsibility' and 'trust' and all that, they took off.

The SECOND Mum and Dad walked out the door, Rodrick jumped up off of the couch and picked up the phone. Then he called every friend he knew and told them he was having a party.

I thought about calling Mum and Dad to tell them what Rodrick was up to, but I've never actually BEEN to a high school party before, so I was curious. I decided to just keep my mouth shut and soak it all in.

Rodrick told me to get some folding tables out of the basement and bring a couple of bags of ice out of the downstairs freezer. Rodrick's friends started to show up around 7.00, and before you knew it, there were cars parked up and down the street.

The first person to walk through the door was Rodrick's friend Ward. A bunch more people started showing up after that, and Rodrick told me we were gonna need more tables. So I went downstairs to get them.

But as soon as I stepped foot in the basement, I heard the door lock behind me.

I pounded on the door, but Rodrick just cranked up the music to drown me out. So I was stuck down there.

Man, I should've known Rodrick would go and pull something like that.

I guess it was pretty dumb of me to think
Rodrick was gonna let me in on the action.

It sounded like it was a pretty wild party.
I think some GIRLS even showed up at one
point, but I couldn't be too sure, because it was
hard to keep track of what was going on from
just looking at the bottoms of people's shoes.

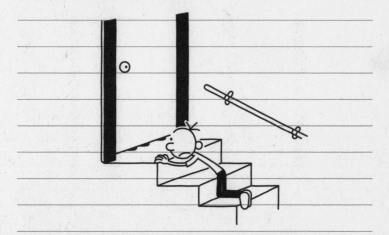

The party was still going strong at 2.00 A.M.,
but that's when I gave up. I spent the night
on one of the spare beds in the basement, even
though there were no blankets on it. I practically
froze to death, but there was no WAY I was
gonna use a blanket from Rodrick's bed.

Somebody must've unlocked the basement door overnight, because when I woke up this morning, it was open. And when I walked upstairs, it looked like a tornado had touched down in the family room.

The last of Rodrick's friends wasn't gone until 3.00 in the afternoon. And once everyone left, Rodrick told me I had to help him clean up.

I told Rodrick he was out of his mind if he thought I was helping. But then Rodrick said that if he got busted for the party, he was taking ME down with him.

He said if I didn't help him clean up the mess, he would tell all my friends about the thing that happened to me this summer.

I couldn't believe Rodrick would play dirty like that. But I could tell he was serious, so I just got to work.

VROOM

Mum and Dad were supposed to be back by 7.00, and we still had a TON of work to do.

It wasn't easy to erase all the evidence of the party, because Rodrick's friends had left trash in all these crazy places. At one point, when I went to make myself a bowl of cereal, a half-eaten piece of pizza fell out of the box.

By 6.45, we had things pretty well wrapped up. I went upstairs to take a shower, and that's when I saw the message written on the inside of the bathroom door.

I tried scrubbing the writing off with soap and water, but whoever wrote that thing must've used a permanent marker.

Mum and Dad were gonna be home any minute, so I thought we were doomed. But then Rodrick had a genius idea. He said we could take the door out and REPLACE it with a closet door from the basement.

So we got some screwdrivers and went to work.

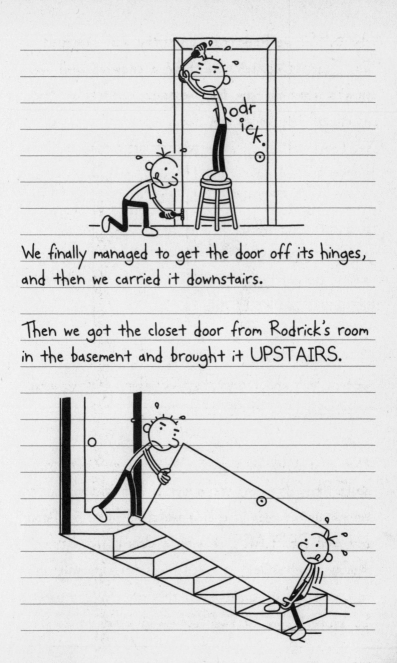

We finally managed to get the door off its hinges, and then we carried it downstairs.

Then we got the closet door from Rodrick's room in the basement and brought it UPSTAIRS.

We made it with no time to spare. Mum and Dad's car rolled into the driveway right when we were tightening the last screw.

You could tell they were pretty relieved the house hadn't burned down while they were away.

I don't think we're totally out of the woods just yet. Because with the way Dad was poking around tonight, I'm sure it won't be long before he figures out about the party.

SNIFF
SNIFF

Well, Rodrick might have lucked out this time, but all I can say is, he should be glad MANNY wasn't there to see the party. Manny is a HUGE tattletale. In fact, he's been telling on me ever since he could talk. He's even told on me for stuff I did BEFORE he could talk.

When I was a kid, I broke the sliding glass door in the family room. Mum and Dad didn't have any evidence that I was the one who did it, so they couldn't peg it on me, and I was in the clear. But Manny was there when it happened, and two years later, he squealed on me.

So after Manny started talking, I had to worry about all the bad things he saw me do when he was a baby.

I used to be a big tattletale myself until I learned my lesson. One time, I told on Rodrick for saying a bad word. Mum asked me which word he said, so I spelled it out. And it was a long one, too.

Well, I ended up getting a bar of soap in my mouth for knowing how to spell a bad word, and Rodrick got off scot-free.

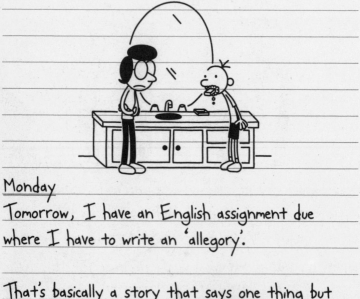

Monday
Tomorrow, I have an English assignment due where I have to write an 'allegory'.

That's basically a story that says one thing but means something else. I was having trouble getting inspired, but then I saw Rodrick outside working on his van, and I got an idea.

Rory Screws Up
by Greg Heffley

Once upon a time there was this monkey named Rory.
The family he lived with loved him very much, even
though he was constantly screwing things up.

One day Rory accidentally rang the doorbell, and
everybody thought he did it on purpose. So they
gave him some bananas as a reward.

Well, now Rory was going around thinking he was some sort of monkey genius or something. And one day, he heard his owner say –

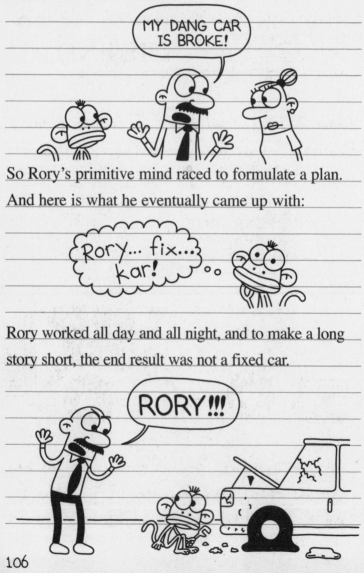

So Rory's primitive mind raced to formulate a plan. And here is what he eventually came up with:

Rory worked all day and all night, and to make a long story short, the end result was not a fixed car.

After it was all over, Rory had learned a very valuable lesson: Rory is a monkey. And monkeys don't fix cars.

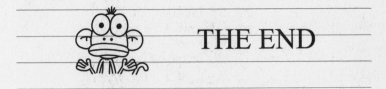

THE END

After I finished my paper, I showed it to Rodrick. I figured he wouldn't get it, and sure enough, I was right.

MONKEYS DON'T UNDERSTAND ENGLISH, STUPID.

LÖDED DIPER

Like I said before, Rodrick knows he's got me under his thumb with this 'secret' thing. So I have to get my licks in any way I can.

Wednesday

Today was Manny's first day of preschool, and apparently it didn't go so great.

All the other kids in Manny's school started back in September. But Manny wasn't potty trained until last week, so that's why he had to wait until now to make the jump from day care.

Manny's preschool was having their Halloween party today, so it wasn't the greatest way to introduce him to his classmates.

Manny's teachers had to call Mum at work and have her come get him.

I remember MY first day of preschool. I didn't really know anyone, so I was pretty scared about being around a bunch of new kids. But this boy named Quinn came right over and started talking to me.

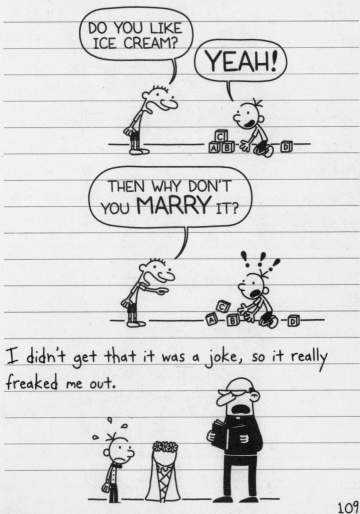

I didn't get that it was a joke, so it really freaked me out.

I told Mum I didn't want to go back to preschool, and I told her all about Quinn and what he said.

But Mum told me Quinn was just being silly, and I didn't need to listen to him.

After Mum explained the joke, I actually thought it was pretty funny. I couldn't wait to go back to school the next day and try it out myself.

But it didn't really have the same effect.

YOU'RE GONNA GROW UP AND GET MARRIED TO SOME ICE-CREAM! HA!

<u>Monday</u>

It's been over a week since Rodrick's party, and I stopped worrying that Mum and Dad were gonna bust us for it. But remember that bathroom door we switched out? Well, I forgot all about it until tonight.

Rodrick was upstairs in my room bugging me, and Dad went into the bathroom. A couple seconds later, he said something that made Rodrick stop cold.

HEY...DIDN'T THIS DOOR USED TO LOCK?

I thought it was over. If Dad knew about the DOOR, it was just a matter of time before he found out about the party.

But Dad didn't put two and two together.

You know, maybe it wouldn't be so bad if Mum and Dad found out about the party. Rodrick would get grounded, which would be AWESOME. So if I can figure out a way to spill the beans without Rodrick finding out, I'm gonna go for it.

Tuesday
I got my first letter from my French pen pal, Mamadou, today. I decided to adjust my attitude and give this whole pen-pal thing my best effort. So when I wrote back to Mamadou today, I tried to be as helpful as possible.

Dear Gregory,
  I am very privileged
to make your acquaintance.
                    Mamadou

Dear Mamadou,

I'm pretty sure 'aquaintance'
doesn't have a 'c' in it.

I really think you need to work
on your English.

                    Sincerely, Greg

I think it's dumb that Madame Lefrere won't
let us use email with our pen pals. Albert Murphy
has already written back and forth with his pen
pal a bunch of times, and it's costing them a lot
of money in stamps.

Dear Jacques—	Dear Albert,	Dear Jacques—
How old are you?	12.	Oh.

COST: $14

Friday
Tonight, Rowley's parents went out to dinner, so they got him a babysitter.

I don't know why Rowley can't just watch himself for a few hours, but believe me I'm not complaining. Rowley's babysitter is Heather Hills, and she's the prettiest girl at Crossland High School.

So whenever the Jeffersons go out, I always make sure to be up at Rowley's for 'story time'.

I went up to Rowley's at about 8.00 tonight. I even splashed on some of Rodrick's cologne to make sure I made a good impression on Heather.

I knocked on the door and waited for Heather to answer. But I was caught a little off guard when Rowley's next-door neighbour Leland answered instead.

I can't believe Rowley's parents switched babysitters from Heather to LELAND. They should've at least checked with me before doing something stupid like THAT.

Once I realised Heather wasn't there, I turned around to go back home. But Rowley asked me if I wanted to hang out and play Magick and Monsters with him and Leland.

The only reason I said 'yes' was because I thought it was some kind of video game. But then I found out that you play it with pencils and paper and these special dice, and that you're supposed to use your 'imagination' or whatever.

It actually turned out to be pretty fun, mostly because in Magick and Monsters you can do all sorts of stuff you could never do in real life.

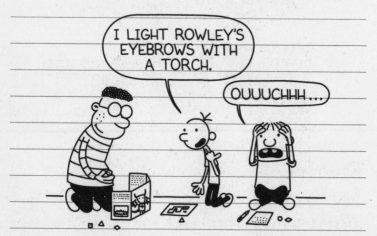

When I got home, I told Mum all about Magick and Monsters and how Leland was a really awesome Dungeon Keeper. Rodrick overheard me talking about Leland, and he said that Leland is the biggest nerd at his high school.

But this is coming from a guy who spends his
Saturday nights putting fake throw-up on people's
cars in the Home Depot parking lot. So I think
I'll just take Rodrick's opinion with a grain of salt.

Wednesday
I've been going up to Leland's house every day
after school to play Magick and Monsters. I was
headed up there again today when Mum stopped
me at the door.

Mum has been acting real suspicious of this whole
Magick and Monsters thing.

And from the questions she's been asking me, I guess she must think Leland is teaching me and Rowley witchcraft or something. So today, Mum said she wanted to go WITH me to Leland's to watch us play.

I BEGGED Mum not to come, because first of all I knew she would never approve of all the violence in the game.

And second of all, I knew that having her in the room would totally ruin the whole experience for everyone.

When I begged Mum not to join us, it made her even MORE suspicious. So now there was no changing her mind.

Rowley and Leland couldn't have cared less that Mum came with me. But I couldn't enjoy myself, because I felt like a total dork playing in front of her.

I figured Mum would eventually get bored and just go home, but she stuck around. And right when I thought she was finally gonna leave, Mum said that SHE wanted to join in the game.

So Leland started setting up a character for Mum, even though I was trying to signal to him that it was a big mistake.

When Leland created a character for Mum, Mum told Leland she wanted HER character to be MY character's mother in the game.

I did some quick thinking and told Mum that all the characters in Magick and Monsters are orphans, so she couldn't be my mother.

And Mum believed me. But then she asked Leland if she could NAME her character 'Mum', and he said 'yes'.

I have to give Mum credit for figuring out that loophole, but it totally ruined the rest of the game for me.

Even though Mum wasn't technically my mother in the game, she sure ACTED like she was.

At this one point, our characters were hanging out in a tavern waiting for a spy to arrive, and my dwarf, Grimlon, ordered a pint of mead. Mead is sort of like beer in Magick and Monsters, and I guess Mum didn't approve of THAT.

MUM ACCIDENTALLY BUMPS GRIMLON'S ARM AND SPILLS HIS DRINK.

The worst part of the game was when we got into a battle situation. See, the whole point of Magick and Monsters is that you're supposed to kill as many monsters as possible so you can get points and move up in levels.

But I don't really think Mum got that concept.

After about an hour of things going like this, I
decided to quit. So I gathered up my stuff, and
me and Mum headed home.

On the way back, Mum was really talking up
Magick and Monsters, saying how it could help me
with my 'math skills' and stuff like that. All I
can say is, I hope she isn't planning on becoming
a regular at these games. Because the first
chance I get, 'Mum' is getting handed over
to a pack of Orcs.

Thursday
After school today, Mum took me to the bookstore
and bought just about every Magick and Monsters
book on the shelf. She must've dropped about
$200, and she didn't even make me cash in a
single Mum Buck.

I realised maybe I judged Mum a little too quick,
and maybe it wasn't such a bad thing having her
in our group after all.

I was all set to take my new books up to Leland's, but that's when I found out there was a catch.

Mum actually bought all those books so me and RODRICK could play Magick and Monsters together. She said it was a good way for the two of us to work out our differences.

Mum told Rodrick she wanted him to be the Dungeon Keeper, just like Leland. Then she dumped the pile of books on Rodrick's bed and told him to start studying up.

It was bad enough playing in front of Mum at Leland's house, but I knew playing with Rodrick would be about ten times worse.

Mum was serious about me and Rodrick playing together, so I knew I was gonna have to go through with it. I spent about an hour up in my room making up characters with names Rodrick couldn't make fun of, like 'Joe' and 'Bob'.

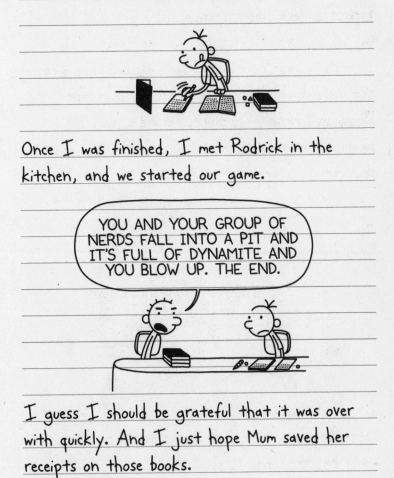

Once I was finished, I met Rodrick in the kitchen, and we started our game.

YOU AND YOUR GROUP OF NERDS FALL INTO A PIT AND IT'S FULL OF DYNAMITE AND YOU BLOW UP. THE END.

I guess I should be grateful that it was over with quickly. And I just hope Mum saved her receipts on those books.

Friday

The teachers have really been cracking down on kids copying off of each other this year. Remember how I said I was glad I got put next to Alex Aruda in Pre-Algebra? Well, THAT hasn't done me any good.

Mrs Lee is my Pre-Algebra teacher, and I'm guessing she also had Rodrick when he was in year seven. Because that woman watches me like a HAWK.

Sometimes I think it would be really cool if I had a glass eye or something like that. First of all, I could use it to play all sorts of wacky tricks on my friends.

But the main thing I'd use it for is to help me get better grades.

On the first day of school, I'd aim my glass eye down like this:

GLASS EYE — REAL EYE

Then I'd go up to the teacher and say, 'Listen, I just wanted to tell you I have a glass eye. So don't go thinking I'm looking at other people's papers.'

OKEY-DOKE. THANKS FOR LETTING ME KNOW.

Then, during a test, I'd aim my glass eye down at my OWN paper, and I'd look at some brainy kid's paper with my REAL eye.

I could copy away! And the teacher would be too dumb to notice.

THAT POOR GLASS EYE KID.

Unfortunately, I DON'T have a glass eye. So if Mum asks me why I flunked my pop quiz in Pre-Algebra today, that's my excuse.

Sunday
Rodrick has been hitting Mum and Dad up for cash lately, so I guess the Mum Bucks program isn't really working out for him. Mum has tried to make Rodrick do more chores to earn some money, but that hasn't been going too well.

IS THIS HOW YOU DO IT?

YOU NEED TO BE USING A CLEAN RAG, SON!

But tonight, Mum figured out a way Rodrick
could earn some cash. My school sent home a
newsletter saying that Music Education has been
cancelled because of budget cuts, so parents
should get their kids private music lessons.

Mum told Rodrick he could give ME private drum
lessons, and that she would PAY him for it.

I think Mum came up with the idea because
lately Rodrick's been telling everyone he's a
'professional drummer'.

There's this local show called the Community
Follies where all the neighborhood parents do a
bunch of comedy skits, and it's been running in our
local theatre for about two weeks.

The other night, the regular drummer got sick, so Rodrick filled in, and he got paid five bucks.

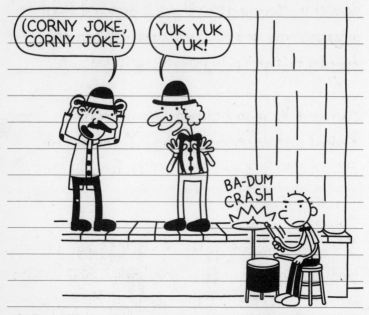

I don't know if that really makes Rodrick a 'professional drummer', but that didn't stop me from using it to score points with the girls at school.

When Mum told Rodrick he should start giving me drum lessons, he wasn't too hot on the idea. But then Mum said she'd pay him ten dollars a lesson, and that I could get a bunch of my friends to sign up, too.

So now I've gotta recruit some people for Rodrick's Drum Academy. And I can already tell, this isn't gonna be a lot of fun.

Monday
I couldn't get any of my friends to sign up for Rodrick's drum school except Rowley, and I kind of had to trick HIM into doing it. Rowley is always saying he wants to learn how to play the drums, but he wants to play the kind they use in marching bands.

I told Rowley I knew for a FACT that Rodrick was going to cover all that stuff in week four, and that got Rowley pretty excited.

I was just glad I wasn't gonna have to take drum lessons all by myself.

Rowley came over after school, and we went down to the basement to start our first lesson. Rodrick started us off with some pretty basic drum drills.

There was only one practice pad and two drum-sticks, so Rowley had to use a paper plate and some plastic utensils. But I guess that's what happens when you're the last person to sign up for a class.

After about fifteen minutes, Rodrick got a call from Ward, and that put an end to our first lesson.

Mum wasn't too happy to see me and Rowley upstairs so soon, and she sent us back down to the basement. She said not to come up until Rodrick had at least given us a practice assignment. So he did.

Tuesday

Me and Rowley had drum lessons with Rodrick again today.

Well, Rodrick might be a good drummer, but he's not a good teacher. Me and Rowley tried our best to do the drills Rodrick taught us, but every time we messed up, Rodrick would get frustrated.

Eventually, he got so fed up that he took our drumsticks away. Rodrick sat down at his drum set and told us to 'watch and learn'. Then he started doing this really long drum solo that didn't have anything to do with the drills he was teaching us.

Rodrick didn't even look up from his drum set when me and Rowley left and went upstairs.

I'm not complaining, though. Because the way I see it, this way everyone wins.

Thursday
We've got a History paper due the day before Thanksgiving, and I'd better start getting serious about it.

The teachers are getting a lot stricter about the quality of work we turn in, and the way I usually do things isn't working so good any more.

Last week we had a paper due in Science, and Mrs Breckman said we had to choose an animal to write about. So I picked the moose. I know I should have gone to the library and done research, but I just decided to wing it.

The Amazing Moose
by Greg Heffley

Diet: The moose eats many, many things, but the list would be way too long to put in this paper. So I will save us all some time by just listing the things that the moose does NOT eat.

BUBBLE GUM   METAL   PIZZA

Even though there are moose habitats set up all over the place, the moose is almost extinct.

Everybody knows the moose evolved from birds, just like people did. But somewhere along the line people got arms, and the moose got stuck with those useless horns.

THE END

I actually thought I did a pretty good job. But I guess Mrs Breckman must be an expert on mooses or something, because she made me go to the library and start the paper over from scratch.

And my NEXT paper isn't gonna be any easier. I have to write a poem about the 1900s for Mr Huff's class, and I don't know the first thing about History OR poetry. So I guess I'd better start hitting the books.

Monday
I was up at Rowley's playing board games yesterday, and the craziest thing happened. When Rowley was in the bathroom, I noticed that there was some play money sticking out of the box of one of the other games.

I couldn't believe my eyes. Because the play money inside that game was the EXACT same kind of money Mum uses for Mum Bucks.

When I counted it up, there was something like $100,000 in cash in that box.

It only took me about two seconds to figure out what to do next.

When I got home, I ran upstairs and stuffed the money under my mattress. I tossed and turned all night trying to figure out what to do with my new Mum Bucks.

I realised Mum would probably have some way of knowing the difference between phony Mum Bucks and the real thing. So this morning, I decided to try a little experiment.

I asked Mum if I could cash in some Mum Bucks so I could buy stamps to write my pen pal. I was really nervous when I handed Mum the money.

But she took it without even blinking.

I can't believe my luck! I figure I can make this $100,000 last all the way through high school, and maybe even further. I might not even have to get a real job later on.

The trick will be to not cash in too much at one time, or Mum will know something's up.

And I have to remember to earn a few Mum
Bucks for real here and there so she doesn't get
too suspicious.

I will say one thing for sure, though, and it's
that I won't be using the money Mum gave me
to buy stamps.

I got a picture from my pen-pal, Mamadou, in
the mail yesterday, and that pretty much killed
any chance of me writing HIM back.

Tuesday

My big History paper is due tomorrow, but they've been saying all week that it's gonna snow about a FOOT tonight.

So I haven't really been sweating it all that much.

At around 10.00, I peeked out the window to see how many inches of snow were on the ground so far. But I couldn't believe my eyes when I pulled back the curtain.

Man, I was counting on school being CANCELLED tomorrow. I turned on the news to see what happened, but the weather guy was telling a TOTALLY different story than he was three hours ago.

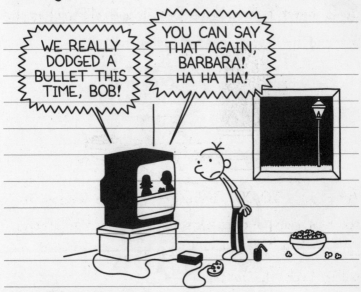

That meant I had to get cracking on my History paper. The problem was, it was too late to go to the library, and we don't have any books in our house that are about the 1900s. So I knew I had to think of something quick.

Then I had a great idea.

Dad has bailed Rodrick out a MILLION times on his school papers. So I figured he could help me, too.

I told Dad about my situation, thinking he'd jump right in and help. But I guess Dad has learned his lesson in that department.

GOOD LUCK WITH THAT!

Rodrick must have overheard me talking to Dad, because he told me I should follow him downstairs.

You know how Rodrick had Mr Huff, my History teacher, in year seven? Well, it turns out Mr Huff gave Rodrick's class the EXACT same assignment when he was in my year.

Rodrick dug around in his junk drawer and found his old paper. And then he told me he'd sell it to me for five bucks.

I told him there was no WAY I'd do that.

I'll admit, it was pretty tempting. Because number one, since all of Rodrick's assignments have gone through Dad, I knew Rodrick got a good grade on his paper. And number two, it was in one of those clear plastic binders that teachers go crazy for.

Plus, I had a huge stash of Mum Bucks under my mattress upstairs, and I knew I could pay Rodrick with that.

But I couldn't do it. I mean, I've copied off of people's papers on quizzes and stuff before, but BUYING a paper off of someone would be taking it to a whole nother level.

So I decided I was gonna just have to suck it up and do the paper myself.

I started doing some research on the computer, but at about midnight, the worst possible thing happened: The power went out.

That's when I knew I was in some serious trouble. I knew I'd flunk History if I didn't turn in a paper. So even though I didn't want to, I decided to take Rodrick up on his offer.

I scraped together $500 in Mum Bucks and went down to the basement. But Rodrick didn't let me off that easy.

Rodrick told me his new price was $20,000 in Mum Bucks. I told him I didn't have it, so he just rolled over and went back to sleep.

At that point, I was really desperate. So I went upstairs and grabbed a big handful of thousand dollar bills and brought them down to Rodrick's room. I gave him the money, and he turned over the paper. I felt really bad about what I did, but I just tried not to think about it and went to sleep.

Wednesday

On the bus ride to school, I took Rodrick's paper out of my bag. But I took one look at it and knew something was seriously wrong.

First of all, the poem wasn't typed out. It was in Rodrick's own handwriting.

That's when it hit me: Dad only started doing Rodrick's papers for him once he got to year NINE. So that meant this paper was Rodrick's OWN work.

I started reading Rodrick's paper to see if I could still use it. But apparently, Rodrick was even worse about doing his research than ME.

A Hundred Years Ago
by Rodrick Heffley

Sometimes I sit and wonder
About stuff I don't know
Like what the heck the earth was like
A hundred years ago.

Did cavemen ride on dinosaurs?
Did flowers even grow?
Well we could guess but that was back
A hundred years ago.

I wish they built a time machine
And they picked me to go
To check out what the scene was like
A hundred years ago.

Did giant spiders rule the earth?
Were deserts filled with snow?
I wonder what the story was
A hundred years ago.

F   See me!

I guess I learned my lesson about buying a paper off someone. Or at least off of RODRICK.

When third period rolled around, I didn't have anything to turn in to Mr Huff. I guess that means I'll be taking summer school for History.

And my day got a whole lot worse after that. When I got home from school, Mum was waiting for me at the front door.

You know that stack of bills I paid Rodrick with? Well, he tried to cash them ALL in at once to get money for a used motorcycle. I'm sure Mum knew something was fishy, since Rodrick has never earned a single Mum Buck on his own.

The rest of the family started trickling in around 11.00. Dad's brother, Uncle Joe, and his kids were the last ones to show up around 12.30.

Uncle Joe's kids all call Dad the same thing.

HI AUNT FWANK!

Mum thinks it's really cute, but Dad swears that Uncle Joe tells his kids to do it on purpose.

Things are pretty tense between Dad and Uncle Joe, because Dad is still mad at Uncle Joe for something he did LAST Thanksgiving. Back then, Manny had just started potty training, and he was doing pretty good. In fact, he was probably about two weeks from being out of diapers.

But Uncle Joe said something to Manny that changed everything.

It was six months before Manny would even step foot in the bathroom again.

Every time Dad changed a dirty diaper after that, I heard him cursing Uncle Joe under his breath.

We had dinner around 2.00, and then people went into the living room to talk. I didn't feel like talking, so I went in the family room to play video games.

Eventually, I guess Dad had enough of the family, too, so he went downstairs to work on his Civil War battlefield. But he forgot to lock the door to the furnace room, and Uncle Joe walked in after him.

Uncle Joe seemed pretty interested in what Dad was working on, so Dad told him all about it.

Dad gave Uncle Joe this big speech about the 150th Regiment and the role it played at Gettysburg, and spent about half an hour describing the whole battle.

But I don't think Uncle Joe was really listening to Dad's speech.

Thanksgiving didn't last too much longer after that. Dad went upstairs and turned up the thermostat until it got stuffy and everyone cleared out. And that's pretty much how Thanksgiving ends every year at our house.

DECEMBER

Saturday

You remember how I said Mum and Dad were going to eventually find out about Rodrick's party? Well, it finally happened today.

Mum sent Dad out to pick up the pictures from Thanksgiving, and when Dad got back, you could tell he wasn't happy about something.

The picture in Dad's hand was from Rodrick's party.

It looked like one of Rodrick's friends accidentally took a picture with Mum's camera, which she keeps on the shelf above the stereo. And when he took the picture, it captured the whole scene.

SAT OCT 27

Rodrick tried to deny that he had a party. But everything was right there in the picture, so there really wasn't any point.

Mum and Dad took away Rodrick's car keys and told him his punishment is that he's not allowed to leave the house for a whole MONTH.

They were even mad at ME, because they said I was Rodrick's 'accomplice'. So I got hit with a two-week video game ban.

Sunday
Mum and Dad have been all over Rodrick's case ever since they found out about his party. Rodrick usually sleeps until 2.00 in the afternoon on weekends, but today Dad made Rodrick get out of bed by 8.00 A.M.

Making Rodrick get out of bed early is a pretty big blow to him, because Rodrick LOVES to sleep. One time last winter, Rodrick slept for thirty-six hours STRAIGHT.

He slept all the way from Sunday night until Tuesday morning, and he didn't even realise he missed a whole day of his life until Tuesday night.

But it looks like Rodrick has found a way around the new 8.00 rule. Now, when Dad tells Rodrick to get out of bed, Rodrick just drags his stuff upstairs with him and he sleeps on the couch until it's time for dinner. So I guess you gotta give this round to Rodrick.

<u>Tuesday</u>
Mum and Dad are going away again this weekend, and they're dropping me and Rodrick off at
Grandpa's. They said they WERE gonna let us
stay home, but we proved we can't be trusted on
our own.

Grandpa lives over in Leisure Towers, which is
this old folks' home. I had to spend a week
there with Rodrick a few months ago, and it was
the low point of my whole summer.

Manny is staying with Gramma this weekend, and
I'd give ANYTHING to trade places with him.
Gramma always has her fridge stocked with soda
and cake and stuff like that, and she has cable
TV with all the movie channels.

The reason Manny is going to Gramma's is because Manny is Gramma's favourite. And all you need to do is take one look at her fridge for the proof.

But if anyone ever accuses Gramma of showing favourites, she gets all defensive.

I LOVE ALL MY GRANDCHILDREN THE SAME.

And it's not just the pictures on the fridge, either. Gramma has Manny's drawings and stuff hanging up all over the house.

The only thing that Gramma has from ME is this note I wrote her when I was six. I was mad at her because she wouldn't give me any ice-cream before dinner, so here's what I wrote:

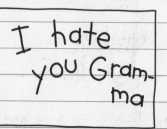

Gramma has kept that note all these years, and she's STILL holding it over my head.

I guess every grandparent has their favourite, and I can understand that. But at least Grandpa is upfront about it.

Saturday
Well, Mum and Dad dumped me and Rodrick off at Grandpa's today, just like they said they were gonna do.

I started looking for ways to entertain myself, but there's nothing in Grandpa's condo that's fun to do, so I just sat down with him and watched TV. But Grandpa doesn't even watch real shows. He just keeps his TV tuned to the security camera that's in the front lobby of his building.

And after a few hours of THAT, you start to go a little nuts.

At about 5.00, Grandpa made us dinner. Grandpa makes this awful thing called 'watercress salad', and it's the worst thing you ever tasted.

It's basically a bunch of cold green beans and cucumbers floating in a pool of vinegar.

Rodrick knows I hate watercress salad more than ANYTHING, so the last time we stayed at Grandpa's, Rodrick made sure to pile it on my plate.

I had to sit there and choke down every bite so Grandpa's feelings wouldn't be hurt.

And guess what I got as a reward for cleaning my plate?

Tonight, Grandpa gave us our salad, and I acted like I was gonna eat it. But then I just stuffed it all in my pocket when noone was looking.

It felt pretty disgusting when the cold vinegar started running down my leg, but believe me it was about a thousand times better than having to EAT it.

After dinner, the three of us went into the living room. Grandpa has all these really old board games, and he always makes me and Rodrick play them with him.

He has this one game called 'Gutbusters', where one player reads a card, and the other player tries not to laugh.

I always beat Grandpa, mostly because the jokes don't make any sense to me.

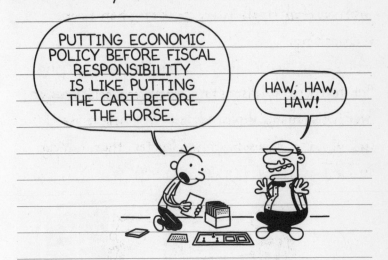

I always beat Rodrick, too, but that's because Rodrick loses on purpose. Whenever it's my turn to read a card, he makes sure he has a big mouthful of milk.

At 10.00, I was ready for bed. But Rodrick called the couch, and that meant I had to sleep with Grandpa again.

All I can say is, if Mum and Dad were trying to teach me a lesson for covering for Rodrick, well, mission accomplished.

Sunday

Rodrick has a big Science Fair project due right before Christmas break, and it looks like Mum and Dad are making Rodrick do this one all by himself.

Last year, Rodrick's science project was called, 'Does Watching Violent Movies Make People Think Violent Thoughts?'

I guess the idea was to have people watch horror movies and then draw pictures afterward to show how the movies affected them.

But it was really just an excuse for Rodrick and his friends to watch a bunch of horror movies on school nights.

Rodrick's friends got the movie-watching part done, but they didn't draw a single picture. And the night before the Science Fair, Rodrick didn't have anything to show for himself.

So me, Mum, and Dad had to bail Rodrick out. Dad typed up the paper, Mum made the poster board stuff, and I had to draw a bunch of pictures.

I did my best to imagine what teenagers would draw after watching violent movies.

The thing that REALLY stinks is that I caught heat from Mum when she saw my drawings, because she said they were 'disturbing'. And that's why I was only allowed to watch G-rated movies for the rest of the year.

But if you want to talk about 'disturbing', you should've seen some of the stuff Manny was coming up with those days.

One night, Rodrick accidentally left one of his
horror movies in the DVD player, and when
Manny went to turn on cartoons the next day,
he got Rodrick's movie instead.

I came across a couple of Manny's drawings
after that, and some of them were enough to
give ME nightmares.

Tuesday

Mum and Dad set up due dates for Rodrick on his Science Fair project, and by 6.00 tonight, he was supposed to tell them the theme of his experiment.

But at 6.45, things weren't looking so good.

Rodrick was watching a show about astronauts, and what happens to them after they've been up in space for a long time. The show said that when the astronauts get back to Earth, they're actually TALLER than when they left.

And the reason is because there's no gravity in space, so their spines decompress or something.

Well, that gave Rodrick the idea he was looking for.

Rodrick told Mum and Dad he was going to do his science experiment on the effect of 'zero gravity' on the human spine. And from the way Rodrick was talking it up, you'd think the results of his experiment were gonna benefit mankind.

Dad seemed pretty impressed. Or maybe he was just relieved that Rodrick actually came through on his first task. But I think Dad started to see things a little different later on when he told Rodrick to take the trash out to the curb.

Wednesday

Yesterday at school, they announced tryouts for the big Winter Talent Show.

As soon as I found out about it, I came up with this AWESOME idea for a comedy skit that me and Rowley could do. But I admit the REAL reason I wrote it was to give myself an excuse to talk to Holly Hills, who is Heather Hills's sister and the most popular girl in my year.

The End.

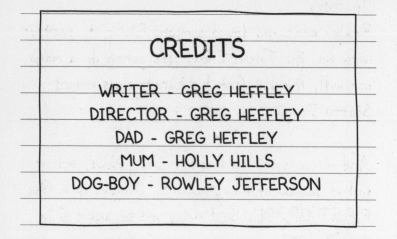

CREDITS

WRITER - GREG HEFFLEY
DIRECTOR - GREG HEFFLEY
DAD - GREG HEFFLEY
MUM - HOLLY HILLS
DOG-BOY - ROWLEY JEFFERSON

I showed Rowley the script, but he wasn't too enthusiastic about the idea.

SHOVE

You'd think Rowley would be grateful that I was gonna make him a big star. But like Mum always says, there are some people you just can't please.

176

Thursday
Rowley went and found someone ELSE to partner
with for the Talent Show. He's gonna do a magic
act with this kid from his karate class named
Scotty Douglas.

And if you want to know if I'm jealous, let me
put it to you this way: Scotty Douglas is in the
FIRST GRADE. So Rowley will be lucky if he
doesn't get beat up at school for this.

They're having one big Talent Show for
primary school and high school. So that
means Rodrick and his band are gonna be
in the same competition as Rowley and
Scotty Douglas.

Rodrick's ALL fired up about the Talent Show.
His band has never played in front of a crowd,
so they see this as their big chance to get noticed.

Rodrick is still grounded, but the rule is that he's not allowed to leave the house. So his band just comes over every day and practises down in the basement. I think Dad's starting to wish he had worded Rodrick's punishment a little differently.

BA-DUM BUM
CRASH BAM

But if Rodrick's band really thinks they can win this Talent Show, they better get serious and play some actual music. Because they spent their last two practices fooling around with a new echo pedal they got over the weekend.

SOMEBODY
FARTED FARTED
FARTED FARTED
FARTED

Friday

Dad ended Rodrick's punishment two weeks early, because he was going bonkers listening to Löded Diper practise every day. So tonight, Rodrick went to his friend Ward's for the weekend.

With Rodrick out of the house, that meant the basement was free. So I invited Rowley over to spend the night.

Me and Rowley bought a bunch of candy and soda, and Rowley brought over his portable TV. We even managed to get our hands on a couple of Rodrick's horror movies, so we were all set. But then Mum came downstairs with Manny.

LOOK WHO CAME TO **JOIN** YOU!

The only reason Mum dumped Manny on us was so he could spy and tell her if we were doing anything wrong.

Every single time I've had a sleepover, Manny has ruined it. The last time Rowley slept over was the WORST.

Manny must've gotten cold in the middle of the night, so he crawled into Rowley's sleeping bag to get warm.

That freaked Rowley out enough to make him go home early. And he hasn't been back to spend the night ever since.

It looked like Manny was gonna ruin ANOTHER sleepover. Me and Rowley couldn't watch our horror movies with Manny around, so we decided to just play board games instead.

But I'm a little of sick of board games, and besides, Rowley was kind of driving me crazy.

He needed to go to the bathroom every five minutes, and whenever he'd come back downstairs, he'd kick a pillow across the room.

It might have been funny the first couple of times, but then it really started getting on my nerves. So the next time Rowley went upstairs to use the bathroom, I played a prank on him.

I put one of Dad's dumbbells underneath a pillow.
And sure enough, the next time Rowley came
downstairs, he gave it a big kick.

Well, that did it. Rowley started blubbering like
a baby, and I couldn't quiet him down.

And with all the racket Rowley was making, Mum
came downstairs.

Mum took a look at Rowley's big toe, and she
seemed pretty concerned. I think Mum's
sensitive about Rowley getting injured in our
house after the tinfoil ball incident, so she
drove him right home.

I was just glad she didn't ask us how it happened.

As soon as Mum and Rowley walked out the door, I knew I'd better start working on Manny.

Manny saw me put that dumbbell under the pillow, and I knew he would tell Mum what I did. So I came up with an idea to keep him from snitching.

I packed some bags and told Manny I was gonna run away from home so I didn't have to face Mum for what I did.

Then I walked out the door and acted like I was leaving for good.

GOOD-BYE, OH, FAMILY. GOOD-BYE, GOOD-BYE, GOOD-BYE!

I got that idea from Rodrick. He used to pull the same kind of thing on me when HE did something bad and he knew I was gonna tell on HIM. He would act like he was running away, and then five minutes later, he would just walk back inside.

And by that time, I was ready to forgive him for whatever he did.

So after I told Manny I was leaving home, I shut the door and waited outside for a few minutes. And when I opened the door, I expected to find him crying in the foyer. But Manny wasn't where I left him. I started walking around the house looking for him, and guess where he was?

Down in the basement, eating my candy.

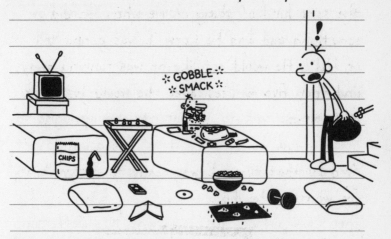

Anyway, if letting Manny eat my candy is the price I have to pay to keep him quiet, I can live with it.

Saturday
After I woke up this morning, I went down to the kitchen. But one look at Mum's face told me that Manny sold me out.

Manny told Mum everything. He even told her
about our horror movies. Don't even ask me how
he knew about THAT.

Mum made me call Rowley to apologise, but then
she made me talk to his parents and apologise to
THEM, too. So I don't think I'm going to get
invited back over to Rowley's house any time soon.

Then Mum got on the phone with Mrs Jefferson.
Mrs Jefferson said Rowley's big toe was broken,
and that he had to stay off it for a week.

Then Mrs Jefferson said Rowley is 'heartbroken',
because this means he'll have to miss the Talent
Show tryouts. And he's been practising his magic
act with Scotty Douglas all week.

So Mum told Mrs Jefferson that I would be HAPPY to fill in for Rowley at the tryouts. I started tugging at Mum's sleeve to let her know this was a TERRIBLE idea, but of course she just ignored me.

After Mum got off the phone, I told her the last thing I needed at school is to be onstage doing magic tricks with a kid who was in pull-ups a year ago.

But Mum made me go through with it anyway. She took me down to Scotty's house and explained the situation to his mother. So now there was no getting out of it.

Mrs Douglas invited me inside, and me and
Scotty went up to his room to start practising.
Well, the first thing I found out was that
Rowley and Scotty were not equal partners in this
act. Rowley was actually Scotty's ASSISTANT.

I told Scotty there was no WAY I was gonna
be a magician's assistant to a first-grader. But
Scotty said it was HIS magic set, and he started
throwing a big tantrum.

So I just went along with the idea to keep
Scotty quiet, because believe me, I did not need
any more trouble.

Then Scotty handed me this shirt that was covered
with all these sparkly sequins, and he told me
that it was my costume.

It looked like something Gramma would wear to Bingo. I told Scotty maybe I could wear something cooler, like a leather jacket, but he said that wouldn't be 'magic' enough.

Anyway, it turns out all I have to do for the act is hand Scotty a prop every once in a while, so maybe it really isn't going to be all that bad.

But ask me how I feel again if we get in and have to perform onstage in front of five hundred people instead of Scotty's baby sister.

Sunday
I'll tell you ONE good thing that's come out of practising this magic act with Scotty Douglas: it's given me a bunch of good ideas for more Creighton the Cretin comics.

Rowley quit doing his comic strip *Zoo-Wee Mama!* for the school paper a few months ago, because he said he wanted to have more time to play with his Dinoblazer action figures. That means the cartoonist job is open again, and maybe I have a shot.

Monday

Well, good news on the Talent Show. The tryouts were today, and me and Scotty didn't make it in.

OK, so maybe I could have done a better job as Scotty's assistant. But I didn't blow it on PURPOSE. I just forgot to hand him his props once or twice.

We were the ONLY ones who didn't make the cut, and that actually is kind of embarrassing.

I know we weren't exactly the best act trying out today, but we weren't the WORST, either. Some of the acts that got in were a lot lamer than our magic act.

This kindergartner named Harry Gilbertson made the cut, and all he did was roller-skate figure eights around a boom box that was playing 'Yankee Doodle Dandy'.

Rodrick's band made it in, too, and he's acting like that's some huge accomplishment.

Like I said before, Rodrick is really excited about the Winter Talent Show. In fact, he actually got his Science Fair project done a day EARLY so he could squeeze in some extra band practises before the big night.

But when Rodrick turned in his project, his Science teacher told him he was gonna have to start over and come up with a whole new idea. He said that Rodrick didn't use the 'scientific method' with a hypothesis and a conclusion and all that.

Rodrick told the teacher he actually grew a sixteenth of an inch during his 'zero gravity' experiment, so that proved he was on to something.

But his teacher said that's a normal amount for a boy Rodrick's age to grow in a month.

Well, this really stinks for me, because I had decided to do my Science Fair project on 'zero gravity', too.

And now it looks like all the research I did was just a big waste of time.

Dad told Rodrick he's going to have to just skip the Talent Show so he can do a new experiment, but Rodrick says he's not going to do it.

Rodrick told Dad he doesn't CARE about school any more. He said his plan is to win the talent show and use the tape of the performance to get signed to a record label. Then he'll quit school and just do the band full-time.

It sounds like a terrible plan to me, but I think Dad is pretty open to the idea.

Wednesday

Tonight was the big Winter Talent Show. I didn't want to go, and neither did Dad. But Mum made us both go to show our support for Rodrick.

Rodrick and Mum went to the school early to bring some stuff that Rodrick's band needed, so Dad had to ride in the band's van with Bill. And Dad wasn't too thrilled when he ran into his boss in the school parking lot.

The show kicked off at 7.00, and let me just say, I think it was a really bad idea to combine primary and high school for this thing.

They ended up having kindergartners singing songs to their teddy bears followed by eighteen-year-olds doing speed metal guitar solos.

AND NOW FOR LARRY LARKIN'S PERFORMANCE OF 'CARNAGE'.

SCOOT SCOOT

I don't think Dad approved of Larry Larkin and all his piercings. Halfway through Larry's guitar solo, Dad leaned over and whispered to the man sitting next to him.

WHAT'S THE WORST THING THAT KID UP THERE COULD SAY TO YOU?

WHAT?

I wish I had time to warn Dad that the guy
he was talking to was Larry's father.

'HI, DAD!'

Another problem with combining the schools was
that there were too many acts, and the show
went on FOREVER.

At 9.30 they decided to start running two acts
at the same time to keep the show moving along.
Sometimes it worked out all right, like when they
had Patty Farrell tap-dancing while Spencer Kitt
was juggling. But other times it didn't work out
too good, like when Terrence James played a
harmonica on a unicycle while Charise Kline read
her poem about global warming.

Rodrick's band was the last act to take the stage.

Before the show, Rodrick asked me to videotape his band during their act, but I told him no WAY.

He's been such a jerk to me lately that I can't believe he was trying to hit me up for a favour. So Mum volunteered for camera duty.

Rodrick's band got paired up with Harry Gilbertson, the roller-skating kid. And I'm sure Rodrick wasn't too happy about THAT.

I noticed Dad wasn't sitting next to me while Rodrick's band played, so I looked around for him.

Dad was standing in the back of the gym with cotton balls sticking out of his ears, and he stayed there until the song was over.

After Rodrick's band performed, they handed out the awards. Rodrick's band didn't win anything, but Harry Gilbertson walked away with the prize for 'Best Musical Act'.

But you'll never guess who the Grand Prize Winner was: Rowley's babysitter, Leland.

He won for his ventriloquist act, because the judges said it was 'wholesome'.

I never thought I'd agree with Rodrick on anything, but I'm starting to wonder if maybe he was right about Leland being a nerd after all.

After the show, Rodrick's band came back to our house to watch the videotape of their performance.

They were all grumbling about how they got 'robbed', and how the judges don't know the first thing about rock and roll.

So their plan was to just mail the videotape off
to some record labels and let their performance
speak for itself.

They all sat down in front of the TV and
Rodrick put the tape in the machine. But it took
about thirty seconds for everyone to realise the
tape was worthless.

You know how Rodrick asked Mum to videotape the
show? Well, she did a pretty good job of filming, but
she talked nonstop during the first two minutes. And
the camera picked up every little comment she made.

THAT SHIRT MAKES
RODRICK'S ARMS LOOK
SO SKINNY!

Every time Bill stuck out his tongue and flicked it up and down like a rock star, you could hear Mum ring in with her opinion.

I DON'T LIKE THAT!

In fact, the only time Mum stopped talking was when Rodrick did his drum solo. But during that part, the camera was shaking around so much that you couldn't even see anything.

At first, Rodrick and his bandmates were really mad. But then one of them remembered that the school taped the Talent Show, and it's supposed to be on the local cable channel tomorrow night.

I guess that means they'll all be coming back over to watch THAT.

Thursday

Well, things have gotten REALLY bad for me in the last few hours.

Rodrick and his bandmates came over around 7.00 tonight to watch the Talent Show on TV. They sat through the whole three-hour show until their band came on.

The school actually did a decent job of taping the performance, and things were looking pretty good up until Rodrick's drum solo.

That's when Mum started dancing. And whoever was doing the filming zoomed right in on Mum, and kept the camera pointed at her for the rest of the song.

SNAP SNAP SECURITY

That meant Rodrick didn't have ANYTHING he could send to record companies. And he was really mad about it, too.

At first he was mad at Mum for messing things up. But Mum said that if Rodrick didn't want people to dance, he shouldn't play music.

Then Rodrick turned on ME. He said this was all MY fault, because if I just taped the show like he asked me to, none of this would've happened.

But I told him that maybe if he wasn't such a jerk, I would have done it for him.

We started to yell at each other. Mum and Dad broke us up, and then they sent Rodrick down to his room and me up to mine.

But a couple of hours later I went downstairs, and I ran into Rodrick in the kitchen. He was smiling, so I knew something was up.

Rodrick told me my 'secret was out'.

At first, I didn't know what he was talking about. But then I got it: he was talking about the thing that happened to me this summer.

I ran down to the basement, and I picked up Rodrick's phone to see if he had made any calls. And sure enough, it looked like he had called EVERY friend of his who had a brother or sister my age.

By tomorrow morning, EVERYONE at my school will know the story. And I'm sure Rodrick exaggerated the facts to make the story sound even WORSE.

Now that my secret's out there, I want to put on record what REALLY happened, and not Rodrick's twisted version.

So here it goes.

Over the summer, me and Rodrick had to stay with Grandpa at his condo in Leisure Towers for a few days. But there was NOTHING to do, and I was going bonkers.

I was so bored, I broke out my old journal and started to write in it. But taking out a book that said 'diary' on the cover in front of Rodrick was a HUGE mistake.

Rodrick stole my journal and made a run for it. He probably would have made it into the bathroom and locked the door if someone hadn't left Gutbusters sitting out.

GAAAH!

TRIP

I scooped the book off the floor and ran out into the hallway and down the stairwell. Then, I ducked into the bathroom in the main lobby and locked myself in a stall.

I kept my feet off the floor so that if Rodrick came in, he wouldn't know I was in there.

I knew that if Rodrick got ahold of my journal, it would be a nightmare. So I decided to just rip the whole thing into tiny little pieces and flush them down the toilet. It was better to just destroy the thing than risk Rodrick getting his hands on it.

But as soon as I started ripping pages out of the book, I heard the bathroom door open. I thought it was Rodrick, so I just stayed completely still.

I didn't hear anything, so I peeked over the top of the stall to see what was going on. That's when I saw a woman standing in front of the mirror, putting on makeup.

I figured the lady just accidentally wandered into the men's room, because people at Leisure Towers are always doing stuff like that.

I was about to speak up and tell this lady she was in the wrong bathroom, but right then someone else walked in. And guess what? It was ANOTHER woman.

That's when I realised that I was the one who messed up, and I was in the WOMEN's bathroom.

I prayed that those ladies would just wash their hands and leave so I could make a run for it. But they sat down in the stalls on either side of me. And every time one woman would leave the bathroom, someone else would come in and take their place. So I couldn't leave.

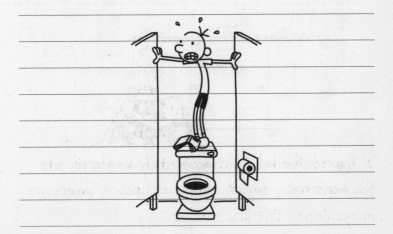

If Rowley thinks he had it bad when those kids made him eat the Cheese, he should try being stuck in the Leisure Towers ladies' room for an hour and a half.

I guess someone eventually heard me in there, and they reported me to the front desk. Within a few minutes, word got around the building that there was a 'Peeping Tom' in the women's room.

By the time security came in and got me out of there, everyone who lived in Leisure Towers was down in the lobby. And Rodrick saw the whole thing unfold upstairs on Grandpa's TV.

Now that the story was out, I knew I couldn't show my face at school. So I told Mum she was gonna have to transfer me somewhere else, and I told her why.

Mum said I shouldn't worry about what other people think. She told me that my classmates would understand that I had just made an 'honest mistake'.

So that just proves once and for all that Mum doesn't understand a THING about kids my age.

Now I'm kicking myself for not keeping up my pen-pal relationship with Mamadou. Because if me and him had stayed in touch, maybe I could have gone to France as an exchange student and hid out THERE for a few years.

All I know is, the one place I don't want to go tomorrow is school. And it looks like that's exactly where I'm headed.

Friday

The CRAZIEST thing happened today. When I walked in the door at school, a bunch of guys cornered me, and I braced myself for the teasing to start. But instead of harassing me, they started CONGRATULATING me.

Everyone was shaking my hand and patting me on the back, and I didn't know WHAT was going on.

With all those guys talking to me at the same time, it took me a while to make sense of anything. But here's what must have happened.

The story Rodrick told his friends got passed on to their brothers and sisters, and then they told THEIR friends.

But by the time word spread around, all the details got totally messed up.

So the story went from me accidentally walking into the women's bathroom at Leisure Towers to me infiltrating the girls' locker room at Crossland HIGH SCHOOL.

I couldn't believe everything got twisted like that, but I wasn't about to set the record straight, either.

All of a sudden, I was the hero at school. I even got a nickname. People were calling me the 'Stealthinator'.

Someone even made me a Stealthinator headband, and you better believe I wore it. Things like this NEVER happen to me, so I wasn't gonna pass up my moment of glory.

And for the first time ever, I knew what it felt like to be the most popular kid at school.

Unfortunately, the girls weren't as impressed with me as the guys were. In fact, I think I might have a little trouble getting someone to go to the Valentine's Dance with me.

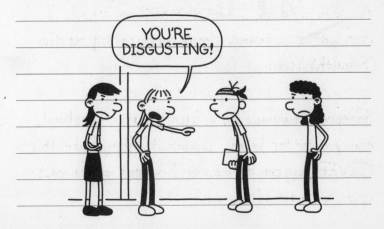

Monday

You know how Rodrick wanted his band to get noticed? Well, he kind of got his wish, because EVERYBODY knows who Löded Diper is now.

I guess somebody must have thought the tape of Mum cutting loose at the Talent Show was pretty funny, because it's all over the Internet. And now everyone knows Rodrick Heffley as the drummer from the 'Dancing Mum' video.

Ever since, Rodrick's been hiding out in the basement, waiting for the whole thing to blow over. And I have to admit, I do feel kind of sorry for him.

I'm getting teased about the video at school, too, but at least I'm not IN it.

And even though Rodrick can be a huge jerk sometimes, he IS my brother.

Tomorrow is the Science Fair, and if Rodrick doesn't turn in a project, he's gonna flunk out of school.

So that's why I offered to help him out with his project, but just this one last time. We worked together all night, and I don't mean to brag, but we did a really good job.

Anyway, when Rodrick gets First Prize tomorrow and passes Science, I just hope he realises how lucky he is to have a brother like ME.

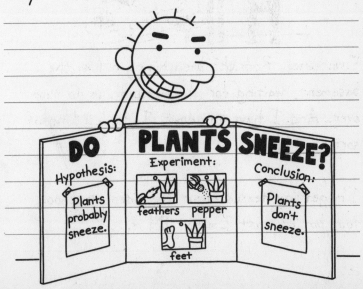

ACKNOWLEDGMENTS

I'll be forever grateful to my family for providing the inspiration, encouragement, and support I need to create these books. A huge thanks goes to my brothers, Scott and Pat; my sister, Re; and to my mum and dad. Without you, there would be no Heffleys. Thanks to my wife Julie, and my kids, who have made so many sacrifices to make my dream of being a cartoonist come true. Thanks also to my in-laws, Tom and Gail, who have been there with a helping hand during every deadline.

Thanks to the terrific folk at Abrams, especially Charlie Kochman, an incredibly dedicated editor and a remarkable human being, and to those people at Abrams with whom I've had the pleasure of working most closely: Jason Wells, Howard Reeves, Susan Van Metre, Chad Beckerman, Samara Klein, Valerie Ralph, and Scott Auerbach. A special thanks goes to Michael Jacobs.

Thanks to Jess Brallier for bringing Greg Heffley to the world on Funbrain.com. Thanks to Betsy Bird (Fuse #8) for wielding her considerable influence to spread the word about *Diary of a Wimpy Kid*. Lastly, thanks to Dee Sockol-Frye, and to all of the booksellers across the country who put these books into kids' hands.

ABOUT THE AUTHOR

Jeff Kinney is an online game developer and designer, and the author of the #1 *New York Times* bestseller *Diary of a Wimpy Kid*. He spent his childhood in the Washington, D.C., area and moved to New England in 1995. Jeff lives in southern Massachusetts with his wife, Julie, and their two sons, Will and Grant.

ALSO BY JEFF KINNEY: BOOK ONE

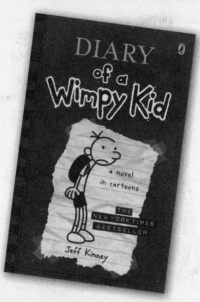

Being a kid can really stink. And no one knows this better than Greg Heffley, who finds himself thrust into high school, where undersized weaklings share the hallways with kids who are taller, meaner, and already shaving.

Luckily Greg has his best friend and sidekick, Rowley. But when Rowley's popularity starts to rise, it kicks off a chain of events that will test their friendship in hilarious fashion.

Praise for *Diary of a Wimpy Kid*:

'[This] "novel in cartoons" should keep readers in stitches, eagerly anticipating Greg's further adventures.' *Publishers Weekly*

'Laugh-out-loud . . . lots of fun throughout.' *Booklist*

ALSO BY JEFF KINNEY, BOOK THREE

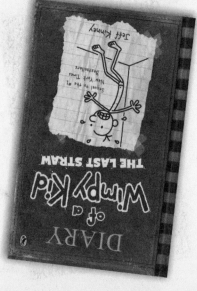

Let's face it: Greg Heffley will never change his wimpy ways. Somebody just needs to explain that to Greg's father.

You see, Frank Heffley actually thinks he can get his son to toughen up, and he enlists Greg in organised sports and other 'manly' endeavours.

Of course, Greg is easily able to sidestep his father's efforts to change him. But when Greg's dad threatens to send him to military academy, Greg realises he has to shape up . . . to get shipped out.

Packed with original art and all-new material,
this Do-It-Yourself Book features ruled pages and
empty word balloons so you can create your own stories
and comics, list your favourites and least faves and keep
your own daily journal. But whatever you do, make sure
you put this book someplace safe after you finish it,
because when you're rich and famous, this thing is
going to be worth a fortune!